"I've Nev...
It's . . .

To her surprise there was moisture in his dark eyes and his voice was husky as he said, "Thank you, Hilary." His voice faltered, and her heart pounded at this evidence that he could feel so deeply. "It's so moving."

For a moment she couldn't trust herself to reply. Remember, she told herself. Remember what he did.

She turned her attention back to the foal, now suckling noisily. "Looks like you've got yourself a filly," she said, keeping her voice as level as she could.

"Looks like I've got myself a new trainer, too. When can you start?"

Dear Reader:

SILHOUETTE DESIRE is an exciting new line of contemporary romances from Silhouette Books. During the past year, many Silhouette readers have written in telling us what other types of stories they'd like to read from Silhouette, and we've kept these comments and suggestions in mind in developing SILHOUETTE DESIRE.

DESIREs feature all of the elements you like to see in a romance, plus a more sensual, provocative story. So if you want to experience all the excitement, passion and joy of falling in love, then SILHOUETTE DESIRE is for you.

For more details write to:

Jane Nicholls
Silhouette Books
PO Box 236
Thornton Road
Croydon
Surrey CR9 3RU

NORA POWERS
No Man's Kisses

Silhouette Desire

Originally Published by Silhouette Books
division of
Harlequin Enterprises Ltd.

*First published in Great Britain 1986
by Silhouette Books, 15–16 Brook's Mews, London W1A 1DR*

© Nora Powers 1986

Silhouette, Silhouette Desire and Colophon are Trade Marks of Harlequin Enterprises B.V.

ISBN 0 373 05256 1

22–0686

*Printed and bound in Great Britain by
Cox & Wyman Ltd, Reading*

NORA POWERS

taught English at the college level while working on her Ph.D. A prolific writer, she is the author of some five hundred pieces of children's verse, fifty-eight short stories, twenty-four novels and various newspaper articles. She has been a published author for the past twenty years and reports, "I don't even recall how I started writing, I was so young."

Other Silhouette Books by Nora Powers

Silhouette Desire

Promise Me Tomorrow
Dream of the West
Time Stands Still
In a Moment's Time
This Brief Interlude
In a Stranger's Arms
A Different Reality

*For further information about
Silhouette Books please write to:*

Jane Nicholls
Silhouette Books
PO Box 236
Thornton Road
Croydon
Surrey CR9 3RU

For Rod and Barb
with love

One

Hilary Benson pushed the battered Stetson back from her forehead and sighed. Jeb had been right to check in with the vet in case he might be needed. Pretty Lady was definitely in labor; it looked like a long night ahead.

Absently she stroked the bay mare's velvet nose. "It'll be all right, girl," she crooned. "You've done this before."

Pretty Lady was no novice at dropping foals. This would be at least her sixth. No, it was not the coming of the foal that put the frown in Hilary's forehead. She wrinkled her nose, which appeared not quite large enough for the rest of her face. It was doubtful that anyone ever noticed that slight deficiency, though, for the gaze did not stop long there; it was drawn to the generous mouth and the wealth of red-brown hair that spilled down her back in a tangle of glorious waves.

"My own little chestnut," her papa had called her when she was small.

Those days seemed so far off now. Hilary sat back on her heels and continued to stroke the restless mare; she was used to delivering foals. There should be no problem with this one. Except that it might belong to Justin Porter III—the dark, menacing stranger who had come from the east, and purchased the neighboring ranch.

Hilary sighed more deeply. Things had been so much simpler before she met Justen. Then the ranch was in the black; then she had papa.

A tear glittered in her eye and she rubbed it away irritably. Papa had been dead for six months, six months since she'd opened the door to find Bruce Kingman in his patrolman's uniform with that uncomfortable look on his face and the terrible news that Papa's truck had run off the road and he'd been killed. He'd been drunk, too, as Bruce was even more uncomfortable telling her.

The mare nudged Hilary, and she realized that she'd forgotten to continue the comforting stroking. "It's okay, girl. Everything will be okay."

The words mocked her. Everything *had been* okay. Till Justin came along. Then everything had gone downhill—rapidly. The terrible debts she hadn't known about until then had put the ranch deeply in the red. They were gambling debts, it was true. But she felt honor bound to pay them.

If only Mama hadn't died. As a young girl Hilary hadn't been strong enough, or wise enough, she thought wryly, to keep a wild cowboy like Papa on the straight and narrow. The tales he'd told of the old days, before he met and married Mama and gave up his wild and woolly ways, had kept her spellbound as a little girl. She'd found it hard to believe that her quiet, hardworking Papa had ridden bucking broncs and wild bulls on the rodeo circuit.

"Take care of him, baby," Mama had said, her pale face composed. "He's a good man."

"Yes, Mama. I will."

Tears spilled over Hilary's eyes and slid unheeded down her cheeks as she remembered those painful moments. She knew about dying. Hadn't she grown up surrounded by the birthing and dying of ranch animals? But this was different. This was Mama who was going to leave her. "I love you, Mama."

"I know, darling. I love you, too. I'm sorry..."

Hilary brushed at her eyes again. "I did the best I could, Mama," she said softly. "I couldn't help it that they sent me away from him."

The bay mare moved nervously, as though Hilary's pain had communicated itself to her. "Easy, girl. Easy."

If only they had let her stay with her father, she thought for the hundredth time. But they had taken her away to live with her mother's parents, the Prescotts, and she had seen her father only for the few brief hours each week when he traveled to Great Falls to visit her. They were wonderful hours, though. Laughing, happy hours they spent together, riding, and talking horses. Dreaming big dreams about the ranch they'd someday have.

The mare moved restlessly. "Not yet, girl," Hilary soothed. "These things take time you know."

Time... Her thoughts drifted back to school. Thankfully her grandparents had let her choose her own career, and she had worked hard at it, learning how to breed and raise horses, learning how to manage a ranch. For always in the back of her mind was the plan that would get her and her father together again.

Texas A & M had not been a picnic of course. The work was hard and she'd had no time for anything but her studies. No time to waste on the boys that were attracted to her red hair and her tall slender body. She had never regretted it, never wished for the starry-eyed silliness that had sometimes overcome her roommates. No man's kisses could keep her from the fulfillment of her plan. Besides, she had been taller than a lot of her male classmates, and somehow, basketball stars had never appealed to her.

From his stall across the stable the chestnut gelding, Brandy, nickered to her. "You'll have to wait, boy. Pretty Lady needs me now. You know that."

At the sound of her name the mare turned such reproachful eyes on Hilary that she had to laugh aloud. "You big baby horse. You know it'll be all right. You've got the easy life now. And you'd better remember it."

The mare whuffled softly and thrust her nose into Hilary's palm. "Okay, okay. I get the idea." She swallowed over the sudden tears. This was the first foal of the season, the first of Golden Boy's offspring. Papa had always been there at her side, his face alive with the miracle of birth. But from now on she would be alone. Jeb was only one man. He had to sleep sometime. She'd been forced to let the other cowhands go. Papa's gambling debts had put the Circle K deeply in the red. She had only kept Jeb on because he obstinately refused to go.

As dusk settled, the stable grew quieter. The shaded bulb shed soft light on the mare's shaggy coat. Absently Hilary pulled at a few loose tufts of hair. Montana winters were cold and the Circle K's horses were put out to graze whenever possible. Yes, Pretty Lady had been with them from the first. Hilary let her thoughts drift back to their first day at the ranch, more than six years ago, the day she'd finally picked up Papa outside the shack he called home and had driven him to the Circle K.

"Do you like it?" she had asked the sun-darkened, bent man who looked so much older than he should.

"It's a neat little spread. Kind of thing your Mama and me was working for." His eyes had clouded over with the old grief.

"The kind of place to raise quarter horses?"

"Sure enough. If a fella had any horses—and cash." He'd looked around. "Maybe when I hit it big next time we'll buy us this place. Is that what you want, baby?"

Triumph had surged through her. "This is our place, Papa. Every bit of it. The Circle K. For Mama."

"My Katherine," he murmured. Then her words seemed to register. "This is our place? How come?"

"There was money," she told him, choosing her words with care; she couldn't lose him now, not when she was so close.

"Money?"

"Yes, Papa. Money Mama left me. I couldn't get it until I graduated from college." A small lie, to save his pride. She hadn't understood why they wouldn't give it to him, but her grandparents had insisted that the ranch be in her name. "So I bought this place." She watched his eyes, eyes darkened by pain.

"You bought this place," he repeated, as though the words had some strange meaning he couldn't fathom.

"Yes, for us. It seemed in pretty good shape. I had to snap it up quick. Someone else was after it."

"So when can you move in?" she asked. "I hope it's real soon. We've got to get some mares. Get them to stud. Next spring we'll have foals of our own."

He stared at her, now really interested. "Girl, are you crazy? We ain't got money for that kind of thing."

"Yes, we do, Papa. There's enough left for maybe three mares. Good stock. And for stud fees. And a little left over to carry us through the first year. We'll have to work hard, real hard. But we can do it. We can make the place pay."

Her eyes scrutinized his face. He had to respond. He had to do this with her. It was for him— this plan she'd worked and dreamed for through the long hard years. For him and for Mama.

"Our own place. To raise horses." His eyes had taken light then, and he became the old Papa she remembered. He looked around and his shoulders straightened. "Girl, we got work to do. Got to get this place in shape. The stable, especially. Take a look at the range. Fix the corral fence." He grabbed her hand. "Let's go get my things. Can't waste no time. Wait." He stopped and shook his head. "You got to get yours."

"They're already here, Papa." She grinned, elated at the success of her plan. "I just couldn't wait."

"That's my girl," he said, returning her grin. "Listen, we got to make some lists. Get—"

"Papa," she interrupted gently. "I went to school, remember? I know what to get." She hurried on. "All but the horses. And the men. You know the men hereabouts. We'll need a foreman, won't we?"

"Yeah, sure." Her father was silent, thinking. "I know just the man for the job, Jeb Stewart. Great cowboy. Knows his horses."

"Yeah," he muttered, more to himself than her. "Nice guy, Jeb. A little strange for a cowboy. Won't touch a drop. But a good guy, anyway."

"Do you know of any good mares for sale?" she asked, joy flooding through her. "And where's the best place to take them to stud?"

"One step at a time, girl. I'm thinking." The gleam in his eyes made her want to laugh with joy. This had been the right idea. It was going to work out. I'm doing it, Mama, she smiled to herself. I'm keeping my promise.

"Let's go get my things," Papa said, eager to get started. "Jess Carter's got a mare, name of Pretty Lady." He snorted, "Damn fool don't know a good horse when he sees one. Stupid jackass scared her so's she won't go into a trailer. Now he thinks she's no good." A grin split his weathered face. "Betcha I can get her cheap. Real cheap."

Hilary grinned back. Papa was the best judge of horseflesh in the West.

And so they'd bought Pretty Lady, got her cheap as Papa had said. And he'd spent the long hours necessary to gain her confidence and remove her fear of trailers.

Hilary absently stroked the mare's withers. Yes, things had been going well. They'd finally got the ranch in the black. Each year a few more mares had been added to the herd. She smiled slightly, thinking how hard it had been for her and her father to part with the young horses. But they had given them the best training possible.

And people had started to come to them for training. Training a horse that they hadn't raised was much harder, of course. There were often problems that would never have occurred if the horses had been raised right. But they did the job and they were good at it. So good that the Circle K and its trainers were getting mentioned in the press, and she got requests to teach seminars on horse management.

If only she could stop teaching them now. Justin was always there, his dark eyes always fastened on her so that she felt as wobbly and weak on her feet as any newborn foal. But much as she hated the seminars, hated the feel of his eyes on her body— the man she had once loved so passionately—she had to go. Because the money she earned there made the difference between buying groceries and not buying them. And unfortunately she still had to eat.

She sighed again. Justin Porter had been the only man ever to get close to her, except for Papa, of course. She had put her trust in Justin, let herself love him and he had let her down.

She *had* loved him! she admitted that to herself. That was why she found it so difficult to see him, to be near him, now. She didn't love him anymore, of course. How could anyone love the man who was responsible for her father's death?

The mare struggled to her feet and went for a mouthful of hay, then came back and lay down again. Her labor was becoming more acute now. The slender hooves of the foal were apparent and, with another look at Hilary, the mare began to grunt loudly. A glance at her watch showed Hilary that it was approaching midnight. With luck the foal would be on its feet and nursing by two or three.

Pretty Lady strained again and Hilary caught a glimpse of a small nose lying along the forelegs.

"Good girl," she soothed. "That's the way. Nice and easy."

Hilary got to her knees, still crooning to the mare, and stretched first one arm and then the other to ease their stiffness.

The creak of the opening door sounded loud in the silent stable. Half turning, her concentration still on the mare, Hilary said, "She's okay, Jeb. I told you to..."

The prickling of the fine hair on the back of her neck warned her before her eyes registered that the shadowy figure in the dimness near the door was too big to be Jeb.

"What are you doing here?" The words tore themselves from her throat with a sound very like a sob.

"I heard my foal was on the way."

As always his voice ran down her spine like an electric charge and her body was filled with an almost unbearable longing to be in his arms. The same longing she'd had to push down and conquer every long cold night since she'd sent him away came close to overcoming her.

She put all the scorn she could into her voice. "You must be psychic."

"Afraid not," he said. "Lafe was at the vet's when your man called in. I thought maybe you could use some help."

"I'm perfectly capable of doing this on my own," she said, turning her eyes back to the straining mare. "Your foal will be all right, *if* it's yours. Go on home."

She sensed that he stopped, that he was fighting a silent battle with himself. Then her heightened feelings told her that he was moving still closer. She wanted to scream at him, Go away! Get out of my life! Haven't you hurt me enough? But she only sat there, on her knees, her hand still moving on the mare's neck.

"I have never doubted your ability with horses," he said dryly. "Though I can't help thinking that with people you're not so good. Take me, for instance."

He stood there beside her, a giant of a man. Insanely, she wanted to lie down in the straw at his feet and weep. To cry out to him, I love you. I love you. The urge was so strong she almost bit through her bottom lip, trying to keep the words back. How could she have such feelings for a man like that? A gambler, a hard drinker. The man who'd killed her father.

He hunkered down beside her as though it was a position he'd used all his life, his jeans stretching taut over his muscular thighs. He was so close she could smell the distinctive after-shave, so close that it was all she could do to keep herself from turning into his arms.

"Take me," he said again. "You persistently misunderstand my intentions. I have perfect confidence in your ability to deliver this foal. And you're probably right in thinking that I'm no use to you at all."

She wished he would stop talking. Even his accent, that hard Boston sound so different from the soft Western drawl she was accustomed to, was a reminder of the ecstasy they had shared, of the love words he had whispered in her ear.

"However, in spite of my lack of knowledge I would like to stay. To see the foal being born. I

promise not to get in the way. If you don't mind my
staying.''

Of course she minded. She minded every painful
moment she spent near him, torn by her desire for
him, buffeted by feelings so strong that it took all
her strength to withstand them. But it would be
good to have someone there. If the mare ran into
trouble, an extra pair of hands could be useful. And
if the foal was a filly, it was his. That had been the
bet and she had to honor it.

"Okay, you can stay." She made the words sound
as gruff as she could. He was a stranger to her now.
An enemy. It was all over between them. "But
you've got to be quiet. If I need help, I'll ask for it.
Otherwise, just sit there."

"Right. And thank you."

As he settled back into the straw beside her, Hilary tried to concentrate on the mare. But the
memory of their first night together, that glorious
night on the summer prairie when she had first
tasted the delights of love, was struggling to reach
the surface of her mind, threatening to engulf her
in feelings so overwhelming that they terrified her.

She stroked the mare and spoke to her sooth-
ingly. "Come on, girl. You can do it."

Again the mare grunted and Hilary saw the out-
line of the foal's head through the membrane sack.

The contractions were much closer now and Hilary spoke soothing, comforting words. Then the
foal's shoulders emerged. With deft fingers Hilary

parted the membrane sack around the little head so that the baby could breathe.

"Come on, girl," she told the mare. "You're almost finished now."

With another sigh the mare began to push again and soon the foal was sliding free.

Hilary sat down on her heels as Pretty Lady put her head down on the straw and heaved a sigh. "It's okay, girl," she said softly, encouragingly. "It's all over now."

"Shouldn't you help it?" Justin asked softly, indicating the red-gold foal that was struggling in the remains of the membrane.

"No. It needs the activity. Besides, the umbilical cord is still attached. It's better if it breaks naturally."

Together they watched, wrapped in silence, as the little bundle that seemed all knobby legs struggled to free itself. Soon Pretty Lady turned her head, saw her baby and whinnied softly in delight.

Hilary chuckled. "Yes, you did it. You got yourself a baby."

The mare began to lick the wet foal and sudden tears shimmered in Hilary's eyes. There was nothing in this world more beautiful than a newborn foal and its mother. A thrill of joy tingled over her. No matter how many times she witnessed it, she always felt the same sense of wonder and of awe at the miracle of birth.

The foal struggled for several minutes before it finally got its spindly legs to hold it erect. Then it tottered over to its mother and began to nurse.

"It'll be all right now," Hilary said. "It was a very normal birth." But not like any she had ever experienced, she thought silently. Having him there beside her, wanting him with an ache that permeated her whole being—that was torture of the worst kind.

The man beside her was silent and finally she turned to him. To her surprise there was moisture in his dark eyes and his voice was husky as he said, "Thank you, Hilary. I've never seen a foaling before. It's..." His voice faltered and her heart pounded at this evidence that he could feel so deeply. "It's so moving."

For a moment she couldn't trust herself to reply. Remember, she told herself. Remember what he did.

She turned her attention back to the foal, now sucking noisily. "Looks like you've got yourself a filly," she said, keeping her voice as level as she could.

"Looks like I've got myself a new trainer, too. When can you start?"

Two

The tension in the stable was so heavy that the mare lifted her head, momentarily neglecting the foal. Scrambling to her feet, Hilary faced him. She stared at him, conscious of the lean body, the broad shoulders, the long legs as he, too, stood up, but even more aware of the grim expression on his handsome face. His dark eyes were determined, and his outthrust chin spoke for itself.

"What do you mean?" She barely managed to get the words out.

"You know what I mean, Hilary. You know the terms of the wager."

"But it wasn't my bet! You know that."

His face turned grimmer. "I hear you've been honoring all your father's gambling debts."

"Of course I have." She glared at him. "He would have paid them." She couldn't let the townspeople talk about Papa. He was dead, but she still loved him. She would pay off every red cent he owed, even though it meant having nothing left for herself.

"Then," he said, his hard Northern voice sharpening the words into icicles, "you should honor this one, too."

"I don't see that that follows." Her knees were trembling and it was not just because she had been down on the straw with the mare for so long. She tilted her head to look up at him, feeling the strength of his attraction to her still and hating it. It was wrong to want this man so much.

"I do." His voice was quiet, but it was deadly. The deep brown eyes that had once spoken so eloquently of his love were shuttered from her now; she could read nothing in them but determination.

"You do remember the wager?" he continued in the same dry tone.

"The foal is yours." If only he would stop talking, she thought. If only he would go away and leave her alone. Hadn't she suffered enough? She was hungry and tired. She wanted to sleep, not to be blown about like a tumbleweed by feelings she couldn't handle, terrible feelings of need. Not to keep thinking of being in his arms.

"There was more to the wager," he went on, as though she hadn't spoken. "Your father was to work for me for a year, to teach me all he knew."

"My father is dead." The words fell between them like stones into a pond. She did not add the next words, though she thought them. *And you killed him.*

The rest of his words faded as her thoughts slipped back in time.

She hadn't wanted him to meet her father yet. Their love was too new, too fragile. She was afraid to risk it. For Justin loved to gamble. Everyone in town knew how he'd play poker at the drop of a hat. He could afford his losses, though. She and Papa couldn't. She knew that occasionally Papa still played. But it was all penny ante stuff, though he had once been a heavy gambler. At least, that's what her grandparents claimed. But not now.

Their love was so precious; she didn't want anything to spoil it. But though she had managed to ignore Justin's repeated hints, she couldn't turn him away when he appeared at the door.

"Papa," she said, taking him into the living room. "This is Justin Porter. I told you about him."

Papa's eyes narrowed shrewdly and she could see him taking inventory. "You ain't from around here," he said finally, motioning to a chair.

"No, sir." Justin folded himself neatly into the chair. "I'm from back East, around Boston."

"You know anything about horses?" inquired her father suspiciously.

Justin's dark eyes twinkled and Hilary let her breath out slowly. "Some, sir. Not as much as you and Hilary, but some." He grinned. "Somewhere back there my mother's people were related to Justin Morgan. That's how I got my name."

Papa nodded. "Neat little horse, the Morgan. But not as good as my quarter horses." His face broke into a big smile. "Nothing's as good as my babies."

"Yes, sir. I'm sure you're right. That's why I'm raising them."

"Listen, young fellow. I don't go fer this 'sir' business. My name's Henry, but they call me Bud. You, too."

"Okay, Bud."

She could see that Justin was enjoying himself. And Papa was clearly taken with him. As she moved toward the kitchen, intent on preparing a pitcher of lemonade and a plate of cookies, she could hear Papa saying, "Hear tell you bought the Dawson place."

"Yes, sir. Bud. Hilary helped me look around. She's been—"

The kitchen door swung closed behind her, shutting off their words, but from time to time she could hear Papa's high laugh and Justin's deep one. Papa and Justin were hitting it off just fine. She hummed as she took cookies from the freezer and spread them out on a plate to thaw. She would just leave the two of them alone for a little while, let them have time to get to know each other. Smiling happily, she took fresh lemons from the refrigerator. She had to wait for the cookies to thaw anyway, and fresh lemonade tasted so much better.

So it was at least half an hour later when she emerged from the kitchen. The sight that greeted her almost made the tray fall from her hands. They had moved to the big dining-room table and on it lay cards. Cards and money. She put the tray down carefully, fighting back an urge to cry. Papa gambling. Right here in the house.

She tried to keep her voice level. "What's going on here?"

"Just a friendly game of poker." Papa's grin was wicked. "Ain't that so, Justin, my boy?"

Justin's grin was just as wicked. Absently, and expertly, he shuffled the deck he was holding. "Yes, sir. Just a friendly game."

"Papa?" She was confused. "I thought . . ." He had never gambled in this house.

Papa frowned. "Don't look so prickly, girl. I just won us the use of Justin's new stallion for a year."

"Golden Boy? Your palomino?" It was like a nightmare. Papa gambling with Justin. How could Justin have done such a thing?

Papa's eyes gleamed. "Yep. But since it was just a friendly game, I'll make you another wager. Give you another chance."

Justin's eyes gleamed, too. "I'm game, Bud. What's your wager?"

"I'll breed all my mares to the stallion this year, like we agreed. If Pretty Lady's foal turns out to be male, that'll be it. I'll raise my own stallion. If not, I get the use of yours for another year."

"Agreed," said Justin promptly, so promptly that Hilary found herself gritting her teeth. "On one condition. If the foal is a filly, I get her and you come to work for me for a year, teach me all you know."

"Ain't gonna be no filly," Papa said. "So it's a safe bet." He pushed himself back from the table and grinned again. "Listen, Justin. It's been a real pleasure meeting you. But I just recollected, I got some things to attend to in town. Some people to see."

And he strutted off, intent, Hilary knew, on getting to his cronies and bragging about how he'd saved the Circle K a year's stud fees and gotten the free services of one of the area's top stallions. To say nothing of having beaten one of Havre's best poker players.

Hilary moistened dry lips. "What...what did he put up against Golden Boy's services?"

"Pretty Lady's next foal." Justin was still grinning. "Actually, I talked him down to that. At first he wanted to bet the mare herself against Golden Boy. I like to gamble, but that seemed a little much. Even for me.''

He moved toward her, big and powerful, the tower of strength she'd been leaning on, the man she had hoped one day to marry. And suddenly he was a perfect stranger to her, suddenly she couldn't bear the thought of him touching her. The man she had trusted so deeply no longer existed. This man, this stranger, had gambled with Papa, pulling him back into the old bad ways. Justin was a hardened gambler himself. He took a another step toward her and she backed away. "Don't!'' she cried, panic overtaking her. "Don't come near me.''

His face registered shock, then pain. "Hilary, what's wrong? Are you ill?''

She shook her head, fighting the urge to scream at him. "No, I'm not. Just go away. Leave me alone.''

He took one more step toward her, but the expression on her face stopped him. With a sigh he turned toward the door. "Okay, Hilary. I'll call you tomorrow. I hope you'll feel better then.''

She wanted to run to him, to fling herself into his arms, to recapture the feelings of trust and joy they had shared. But she could not. Those feelings were shattered, gone forever. She had felt them for a man who never really existed.

"Tell your father to call me tomorrow, before Golden Boy's calendar is filled up,'' he said.

Then he was gone and she was left staring at the plate of untouched cookies and the wreck of her dreams.

"Hilary." The sound of her name brought her back to the present. "You owe me this."

"You're wrong," she said stubbornly. "I don't owe you anything. You killed my papa."

"Don't tell me you're still at that." His voice was hard and clipped. "The old man killed himself. He drank too much." His eyes searched her face. "You know that as well as anyone."

"I know this," she said, biting off her words and spitting them at him. "Papa was okay until you came along. Until you suckered him into that bet."

"I suckered him? You're crazy. He was your father. I wanted to please him."

Sarcasm laced her voice with acid. "You sure picked one hell of a way to do it. It was that bet that started him downhill, that led to his death."

His eyes held real anguish. "And you still hold me responsible for that?"

She nodded. "Yes, I do."

It was that stupid wager that had started Papa downhill again. Hadn't he come home that very same night loaded and singing such a bawdy song that Jeb had to practically knock him out to keep him quiet? And hadn't he come home many nights after that, in the same terrible condition, until the night he hadn't come home at all?

"I know for a fact," Justin went on sternly, "that you're paying off all your father's gambling debts. I don't see why I should be any exception."

"The filly is yours," she replied, her tone as cold as his. "You'll have her as soon as she can leave the mare."

"I don't want her that soon. I want you to train her."

"I . . ." She couldn't refuse him. The filly already had a piece of her heart and she needed the proper training. "Okay, I'll do that."

"Good."

She didn't like looking at him; it was too painful. But she'd be damned if she'd break eye contact first. She fought the surge of pain that hit her.

"I know you're busy here," he said, almost as though he didn't know what Papa's death had done to the Circle K. "So I've been thinking. If you give me three days a week that'll be enough. Your salary will be paid monthly."

"What salary?" She was shocked out of her pain by the thought of money. Money to buy winter hay and oats. Money to pay the vet.

"The salary your father and I agreed on," he said calmly. "A thousand dollars a month."

"But I didn't hear anything about a salary," she protested. Against her will she felt the fluttering of hope.

"You were in the kitchen," he pointed out. "And afterward"—a fleeting expression of pain crossed his face and was replaced by sternness—"afterward there wasn't much chance to tell you anything."

"Which days?" she asked, knowing she shouldn't be near him but not able to refuse the money she needed so badly.

"Whichever three are convenient for you," he replied. "I'm not a monster."

"I have to have full control," she said, her voice brisk and businesslike. "My methods are unusual and they won't work if someone interferes. Maybe half days would be better," she mused. "Horses need to be worked every day."

"If you think that's best," he agreed, his tone brisk and businesslike, too. "That'll give you time to work with Golden Lady every day."

They turned together to where the red-gold foal was nursing while Pretty Lady licked her fuzzy back clean.

"Yes," Hilary said, nodding. "The name fits."

"Well, I'm glad that's decided," Justin said. "I knew I could count on you to do the right thing." He extended his hand. Would she take it? he wondered. Or would she back off like a spooked horse? God, but she looked awful. Big dark circles under her eyes. No flesh on her bones. She was working herself to death. And all because of that father of hers. He longed to take her in his arms, to comfort and care for her. The impulse was so strong that he took another half step forward before he could stop himself.

She took his hand then, shook it briefly and dropped it like a hot potato. Had the touch burned her, too? he wondered. She looked so tired, a mere shadow of the laughing, loving woman he had once known.

Once again he remembered how her body felt under his, remembered the surging passion and their mutual joy. Damn himself for letting her father sway him to play poker. How was he to know she didn't have the word on her father's gambling? Everyone in town seemed to know about it. In point of fact, as a newcomer he had used the town's regular Friday night poker game to gain acceptance, to become one of the boys.

Patience, he told himself. The past is over no use dwelling on it. At least she was talking to him. And now she would be coming to the ranch every day. The old magic would work between them. She felt it now, just like he did. He could see it in her eyes. In the way she held herself.

He felt again the urge to take her in his arms, but he controlled it. He'd already waited nearly a year. He could wait a little longer. He would wait, he recognized with a grim sense of amusement at the realization, just as long as it took. Because this scrawny bean pole that stood weaving on her feet, her faded jeans and jacket covered with straw, her green eyes blurred with fatigue—this was the woman he loved, the woman he planned to marry. He would get her to marry him, he told himself, no matter how long it took. And at least now the long wait for the foal's birth was over. At least now he could have more than the tantalizing glimpses of her that he'd been getting at the horse management seminars.

"Can I expect you Monday?" he asked, trying to conceal his elation.

"Yes." She was still fighting the effects of his touch. It wasn't fair, she thought bitterly. There ought to be some way to cancel the physical feelings when you didn't want them anymore, when they were too dangerous.

"Morning or afternoon?" Justin inquired, his eyes traveling over her.

"Wh-what?" The weariness was getting to her now. She longed to sink down in the straw and sleep.

"Will you be working for me in the mornings or the afternoons?"

She tried to think. "Mornings. Early."

"Fine. I'll see you Monday, then."

He turned and made his way back to the door. She didn't move to go with him: she was not sure she would ever move again. But her eyes followed him, drinking in every little detail, every familiar movement. And then he was gone, closing the stable door quietly behind him.

Her knees did not buckle. She was too strong for that. She stood there for one more long moment before she turned back to the mare. There was the afterbirth to be attended to. And then, maybe then, she could fall into her bed and sleep.

The morning sun was lacing the sky with gold when Hilary finally reached her bed and stretched out gratefully. The mare and foal were both fine. Jeb was starting morning chores. He had insisted that he could handle things while she caught up on her sleep.

This time she had not argued with him. She'd been up all night before and had carried on the next day as usual. But never had she been so mentally exhausted as her confrontation with Justin had left her. Being so close to him, talking to him like that, was a thousand times more painful than seeing him at the horse management meetings. And that had been bad enough.

Her tired mind rioted with thoughts. Now she had agreed to work for the man. She shouldn't have done it, of course. But he was right about some things. She *had* paid all Papa's other gambling debts. And it *was* unfair to make an exception of him. A thousand a month was nothing to sneer at, either, not when there were those loans to be paid off. The money, at least, would be welcome. And she would give him full value for it.

She rolled to her side and curled up. If only she could go to sleep. She didn't need this kind of hassle. There was a lot to be done, and she needed to be clearheaded to do it.

Summoning a picture of the new foal might help. He'd named her Golden Lady. Hilary liked that. It acknowledged both Pretty Lady and Golden Boy. She tried to fill her mind with images of the spindly legged filly, but the effort was useless. Her mind insisted on going back to Justin. How clearly she could see him! The tall powerful body: broad-shouldered, lean-hipped, flat-bellied. He might have been an Eastern businessman when she first met him, new to the West, and looking a little uneasy in his ranch clothes. But he'd also been eager to learn. And now no one could tell that Justin wasn't a born-and-bred cowboy. A little smile tugged at the corners of her mouth. Until he spoke, that is. His time in Montana had not softened the hard New England accent.

Other things had not changed, either, she thought ruefully. He was still like a magnet, drawing her powerfully toward him. She had tried thinking of their attraction in the purely physical terms of stallion and mare, but the analogy would not work. What she felt for Justin went much further than the merely physical. It was true that she still woke many nights longing for his touch, that her body ached for the feel of his, yearned for the tumultuous joy of their lovemaking.

But the other loss was even greater. She missed his quick wit, his mental strength and solidity, his quiet, intense way of listening to her, so that she felt she had every bit of his attention. The comfort— both mental and physical—of having him there. She wanted him still; she was not foolish enough to try to deny it. It was better to face up to problems; running away from them was stupid. But facing up to this problem wasn't going to help. She should not be wanting the man who had pulled her father down. Papa had been doing fine, until he and Justin made that stupid bet and he'd started drinking. Justin was clearly responsible for that terrible, stupid wager. And wasn't he collecting on it, even now?

She shivered in the warm bed as she recollected the touch of his hand on hers. He'd always had that power. Like some kind of short circuit, touching him seemed to affect her thinking, to say nothing of her body.

Justin had been interested in horses and ranching. And soon she'd stopped thinking of his rich Eastern background and treated him like anyone else, giving him all the help she could in realizing his dream of setting up a horse-raising business. She knew, after all those long years of waiting, what a dream could mean. Justin, of course, could go about it in a big way. He could get his own stallion and as many mares as he pleased. It was time that had kept him from his dream—not money. And finally he had found the time to make it come true.

If only they had just stayed friends. But the look in Justin's eyes, the way he talked to her, the way he touched her at every opportunity... She was not experienced, but she *was* female and there was no mistaking his intent.

She moved restlessly, wishing she could forget that first time, wishing it had never happened. But not even all the misery that she'd felt since could dim the memory of that ecstatic night.

"Damn the man!" she cried, sitting up in her lonely bed and angrily shaking her fist at the ceiling. "Damn him for making me hurt like this!"

Three

———

Monday morning came, following a weekend that had done nothing to improve her temper. A thousand times she'd been on the verge of storming into the kitchen, and dialing Justin, to tell him precisely where he could go and take his blankety blank job with him. But a thousand times she'd stopped in her tracks, looked out over the Circle K and known she couldn't do it. Papa was gone, but the ranch that had been their dream was still there. It was all she had left now. The ranch and her horses. And she would do anything to keep them.

Besides, she told herself angrily as she approached the Rocking J shortly after sunrise on Monday morning, she would have to see Justin now anyway. He would want to keep close tabs on the foal. Golden Lady promised to be a big asset to the Rocking J's herd.

As her horse neared the sprawling ranch, Hilary looked around her. It was almost a year since she'd been to Justin's place. Everything looked good; she had to admit that. But, then, Justin had the money to keep things in shape. No scrimping and saving for him. He probably wouldn't even miss the thousand dollars a month he was paying her, while to her it meant . . . She pulled her mind sharply away from that. She'd already gone over the bills and knew to the last penny who was going to get what.

The Rocking J stable looked in tiptop shape, too, she thought as she rode into the yard. The sound of activity inside told her that Justin's hands were going about their duties. She was about to swing down when the distressed whinny of a mare reached her ears. In a second she was off Brandy and dropping the reins to the ground. As she ran toward the stable door another whinny sounded. The mare was really disturbed.

Hilary pushed open the door and rushed inside. At the far end of the stable, where a large door led out into the corral, a ranch hand was tugging at a struggling foal. From a nearby stall the mare's calls became more frantic, and she started kicking wildly at the door. The rustling of straw and the trampling of nervous hooves warned Hilary that the rest of the horses in the stable were reacting to the mare's panic.

"Hold it right there!" Her words froze everything into silence.

The ranch hand turned to stare at her. "Before you ask who the hell I am," she said, grimly advancing on him, "you'd better give me that foal. Then you can go tell your boss that his new trainer is here. From the looks of things, I'm just in time."

She covered the remaining distance between them, confidently took the lead rope from his hand and gave him another grim look. "I want to see Mr. Porter. And I want to see him now."

Then she turned her back on him, dismissing him, and gave all her attention to the foal who was struggling valiantly to return to its mother. "Easy, fellow," Hilary soothed. "We're going."

The mare nickered eagerly as she heard her baby approaching, and Hilary spoke softly as she opened the stall door and led the baby inside. "Easy, girl. Easy. He's all right."

The mare was obviously nervous. Her ears were still shifting and her eyes rolled a little, but she calmed down when she saw the foal.

"Yes, girl," Hilary murmured. "He's all right. No one will take him away from you. Not anymore."

Her fingers trembled with anger as she loosened the halter the colt wore. A baby this age had no business wearing a halter, either. She slipped it off as the mare anxiously inspected her offspring.

"He's okay, girl." Hilary smoothed the mare's flank. This was a new mare, not one of those she had helped Justin buy. But she was a beauty. A pale, claybank dun, her coat looked almost peach. And her foal was similarly colored, with a red stripe down his back.

When she had assured herself that her baby was unharmed, the mare turned to Hilary. "Hello, girl." Hilary breathed softly into the mare's nostrils. "How are you?" The mare whuffled back and Hilary smiled to herself. It never failed—Papa's way of greeting a new horse.

"Stands to reason," he used to say. "You want to be friends with a horse, say hello to him like another horse would."

The stable door flew open with a bang, hitting the wall, but Hilary ignored it, her attention all on the mare.

"What the hell's going on in here?" Justin demanded loudly. "And what are you doing in the stall with that rogue mare?"

So that was it. Hilary turned to him, noting his white shirt and business suit. He must be on his way into town. "This mare?" She put a casual arm around the dun and leaned on her withers. "Nothing wrong with this mare."

Justin's face looked white under his tan. "Get out of there before you get hurt. She's already kicked one hand into the hospital."

Hilary shrugged. "No wonder. I'd do the same if somebody started dragging my baby off."

"Will you stop babbling and get out of there?" God, if that crazy mare kicked her... He wouldn't be able to stand it if she got hurt. Why had he gotten himself tangled up with such a stubborn, foolhardy, crazy... With difficulty he kept himself from rushing into the stall and jerking her out to safety. Jerking her, he thought as he felt his muscles tensing, into his arms. Why couldn't he have fallen in love with some sensible woman instead of this crazy wildcat?

Picking up the foal's discarded halter, she gave the mare one last pat and strolled out.

He slammed the door shut behind her. "Now what's going on?" How could he love someone so damned exasperating? At least she looked a little better than she had the other night. Though the circles under her eyes had faded some, she was still as thin as a rail, and her clothes seemed to hang on her. He would send her the first check soon. He hoped she wouldn't be too proud to accept it before the month was out.

She thrust the halter at him as though it were some instrument of torture. "Look at this!"

"It's a halter. What's wrong with that?"

She glared at him. "That baby doesn't need a halter. He's only a couple weeks old."

"Pete said we'd better leave it on. So we could take him out easier."

"And that's another thing," she said, her eyes blazing. "What idiot gave orders to take this mare's baby away from her?"

"He was taking the colt out for exercise."

"And why weren't they put out to pasture together?" she demanded, as though he had committed some outrageous crime.

"I told you. The mare's a rogue. She attacked a hand."

Hilary fixed him with an angry eye. "How long has she been in this stall?"

He was beginning to feel really uncomfortable. He'd forgotten how deep her feelings for horses ran. "Since she foaled, I guess."

"Justin Porter! This mare is a finely bred, sensitive animal. You can't leave her cooped up like this. No wonder she's acting up. She's bored to death, for one thing. And then someone takes her baby."

"She kicked a hand." Even to his own ears his words sounded weak. He should have paid more attention to what was going on out here. But the past few weeks he'd been unable to think of anything but Hilary.

His face flushed and she felt elation. She was getting under his skin and she liked it. So he wanted to learn about horses? Well, she was going to teach him. "Show me which pasture. I'll take the mare myself." She tossed the offending halter nonchalantly over a nail. "And tell everyone else to keep away."

He flushed again and she saw that little muscle tense in his jaw, the one that meant that he was annoyed. "Then I want all the hands together. I've got a few things to say to them." Her eyes dared him to contradict her.

"Do you have to do that while you're still so..."

"Outraged?" she suggested.

"Upset," he countered, his tone softer than hers. "I just think you might get along better here if you don't dump on everyone to start with."

He was right, of course. She knew that. But she needed this anger. She needed to hang on to it so she could ignore the other feelings that threatened to engulf her. Seeing him, being with him, was so difficult. Every cell in her body clamored for the feel of him. There was a big hole inside her since they'd parted. A vast void that could be filled only by his presence, by his love. But that could never be. She could never be with this hard drinking cardsharp who was responsible for her father's death.

She made her voice as scathing as she could. "The agreement was that I have free rein. You needn't worry about me. Everyone around here knows Paul Benson's daughter. They may not agree with my methods, but they know they work."

She forced herself to meet his eyes, to push down the feelings that pulsed through her. "If I'm going to be the trainer here, things will be done my way. Your ranch hands have got to know that. I don't want anybody sabotaging things behind my back."

She glared at him, fighting down more tender feelings. "And believe me, I'll know if they do. So the word had better get out that I mean business."

She pulled a lead rope from a hook and turned back toward the stall. "And now, tell everyone to get out of my way. I'm taking this *rogue* mare to pasture."

Late that morning as she moved toward the corral where the men had gathered, Hilary was not feeling nearly so sure of herself. Justin had been right about one thing: it was not going to help things any if she immediately alienated all his hands. People were not as easy to deal with as horses—at least not for her. She sighed and straightened her shoulders. This was just one more task in a long full day.

All heads turned toward her as she reached the group. Frankly curious eyes gave her the once-over, this upstart girl. Though she was twenty-eight years old, most of these hands were grizzled old-timers. She was sure they thought of her as a girl and not as a woman. Her eyes searched for and did not find the face of the offending hand, Pete. With any luck Justin had already let him go. At least, she thought, the hands looked more curious than malicious. They would listen to her before they made any judgments.

"I'm Hilary Benson," she said, wanting to get this over quickly and glad that Justin was not in sight. "Some of you knew my Papa." Several heads nodded. "His methods were unusual." A couple of men chuckled. "And he found that it paid off. I follow my papa's ways. I never do anything to cause the horse discomfort, to make things difficult for him."

She looked at each man directly. "Above all I never think of the training process as a contest between man and beast. The horse doesn't have to be conquered, it just has to be taught."

Several faces turned skeptical. "Bad horses," she continued, "are not born. They're caused by bad training. They can be retaught, but that takes time."

"I remember Pretty Lady," said one hand with grizzled hair and weather-beaten face. "Jess Carter couldn't hardly give that mare away. Your daddy got her dirt cheap and he cured her." Several heads nodded in unison, and Hilary felt some of her tension slowly draining away.

"Yes," she said. "And she became one of our best brood mares." She paused. "If I tell you to do it, it works. And that's what Mr. Porter wants."

"That's right." The deep voice sounded from so close behind her that she jumped and almost lost her balance. All her nerves tingled with his nearness, but she refused to turn to look at him as he spoke. "Miss Benson is the boss here. Where the horses are concerned, her word is law."

The hands all nodded. Hilary, watching their faces carefully, could see no signs of anger or resentment. She could almost see them thinking that Bud Benson's daughter deserved a chance. Papa had helped her one more time, she thought gratefully.

She took a deep breath. "Mares and foals are not to be separated. When weather permits, no horses should be kept stabled unless absolutely necessary." She grinned at them. "A properly trained horse will come when you want it."

That reminded her. "No halters are to be left on foals. Tomorrow morning I'll be working with the dun mare..." She paused as several mouths fell open. "That mare is no more rogue than I am," she assured them. "I want everyone who can be spared to be at the east pasture." She chuckled. "Stay outside the fence. *I'll* be safer that way. That's all for now. See you tomorrow."

As the men moved off to go about their chores, Hilary edged toward the stable. If she could just walk away and not have to talk to him, not have to look at him. But Justin wasn't going to allow that. "Wait a minute." His voice stopped her, but she had to fight with herself before she could turn around and face him. She managed it finally. He had changed his clothes on his return from town.

His faded blue jeans molded his strong thighs. His plaid shirt was open partway down his chest, revealing the wisps of curling chest hair that she had once rested her cheek against. She pushed the thought away. "Yes, Mr. Porter?"

"I backed you up in front of my men," he said quietly. "But listening to you just now I'm not so sure your ideas are sound. We can't go around babying the horses."

Hilary snorted. Sometimes he could be really stupid. "Babying! I'm not talking about babying. I'm talking about plain common sense. Who do you suppose will do more for you, your friend or your enemy?"

He looked puzzled. "Your friend, of course. Anyone ought to know that."

"Of course. And anyone *ought* to know that a horse that's a friend will do more for you than one that's an enemy."

Justin looked thoughtful, his dark brows drawing together. "I can see that. But it sounds like you let the horses run things."

"It may sound that way," Hilary replied. "But it isn't so. Take the dun mare's new foal. He's two weeks old?"

Justin nodded.

"Ideally, you should start as soon as the foal's born." She felt that she was babbling, telling him too much, too soon, but she was afraid to be silent, afraid to think anything but horses. He was so close and she wanted him so much. "If the training is done properly, that foal will grow up to be a horse that always works well."

His eyes bored into hers. There was no mistaking the desire that flickered there. Her stomach twisted. She wanted him so much. Not just the sexual part, but the comfort of his love. She felt so terribly alone.

She'd never had a lot of friends, even as a child. And her college years had been one long stretch of hard work, fighting against time to get back to Papa. But Justin had changed all that. Justin had filled all the empty spaces in her soul, spaces she hadn't even known were there because he had filled them so well.

But now she knew they were there. Now she knew the ache of missing him, an ache that felt as though she were missing part of her own self. Nothing was right anymore. The days were long hours of hard, unremitting labor. The nights were endless hours of emptiness and pain. The emptiness of not having him.

"I want to understand all this," Justin was saying. "I believe you know what you're doing. Your reputation is very good."

Hilary nodded. Think about horses, she told herself. Think about ranching. Think about anything except Justin and the way it feels to be in his arms. "So they tell me." She looked at her watch. "Now, if you don't mind, the morning is over. It's time I got home. Jeb can't handle everything, you know.''

"I know." His tone denied the accusation in her words. "But it is part of our deal that you teach me." He raised a hand to still her protest. "I need to understand *why* you do the things you do, not just *what* you do. And to understand I need to talk to you.''

"Our agreement is for mornings," Hilary protested.

"You do eat, don't you?" he asked.

"Of course I eat," she said.

"Good. Then come up to the house and have lunch with me.''

"I . . ." She cast about in her mind for some excuse, but she could think of nothing, nothing but the times they had shared a table for dinner, shared their thoughts and their dreams, and later shared their bodies. Warmth flooded over her.

"It'll save you time in the long run," he pointed out smoothly. "That way you can go right home and get to work.''

There wasn't any way she could refute that. Not unless she told him that she seldom ate lunch. And somehow she couldn't do that. "Well, all right, but I can't linger. Not if you want your filly to be properly trained.''

"Agreed," he said. "Come along then. Cookie has it ready for the table exactly at noon. And if I'm not there . . .''

"Right," she replied, glad to have something neutral to talk about. "Cooks can be petty tyrants."

Minutes later she had washed her face and hands and was seated across from him. Horses, she told herself, think about horses. Talk about horses. But it was not easy. He was so close.

His dark eyes showed signs of strain. There were new worry lines around them. She wondered how things had been for him this past year. The ranch looked prosperous enough and the horses were all in good shape. It must be something else that made him look older and tired.

She fought down an urge to lean across the table and touch his hand. It had always been strong, his hand. Now it was baked brown by the sun, like any rancher's hand. The sun had darkened his face, too, but that only made him look more handsome. She swallowed a sigh. Justin was everything she had always wanted in a man. If only he hadn't come to the ranch that afternoon, if only she hadn't left them alone. But it would have happened sometime. Didn't gamblers like Justin always manage to find a way to get a game going? She shifted uneasily in her chair.

Across the table from her, Justin spoke. "Tell me about horses," he said. "Start at the beginning."

"Some of it I've told you before," she pointed out, wanting only to get away from him.

"That doesn't matter. It's important to me to understand."

She nodded. At least horse talk filled the time. "Horses are very intelligent," she began. "They have phenomenal memories, especially for those who hurt them."

Justin smiled slightly. "I thought that was just in stories."

Hilary shook her head. "No, it's very true. A lot of what you read about horses is silly, but that's one thing that's true. They can sense how you feel about them. They know if you're afraid, too. Or if you dislike them."

Justin nodded. "I can believe that readily enough."

"Yes." Hilary nodded. "That's why horses don't hurt little kids when they climb around between their legs. They know the kids aren't afraid and they know, somehow, that they're young, that they're just babies."

Justin looked slightly skeptical.

"I don't know how they know," she continued, as the cook, a big cowboy wearing a white apron, set bowls of hearty beef stew in front of them. "But I've seen the friskiest animal walk with the greatest care when he had a youngster on his back."

"All right, I guess I can buy that." Justin's dark eyes met hers. "But it did seem to me that you got a little carried away this morning. Pete was only taking the foal for a little walk."

Hilary shook her head. "The mare didn't know that. Horses are intelligent, but they can't read minds. Morning Glory only knew that someone took her foal. She had no way of knowing that they'd bring it back.

"You make sense," Justin said. "Especially when you explain the reasoning behind things." He gazed down at his bowl. "We'd probably better suspend our discussion until we've finished this. Cookie doesn't like to have his efforts get cold."

Hilary nodded and picked up her fork. The stew smelled divine and her stomach was already reminding her how long it had been since her scanty breakfast. It was one thing to skip lunch by telling herself that she was too busy and that the pantry shelves were bare. It was quite another when a savory dish like this was set right under her nose. She dug in with a will, for the moment forgetting everything but the satisfaction of eating good food. This was one plus to the job that she hadn't considered.

She finished the stew and leaned back, contentedly. "Give my compliments to Cookie," she said. "I've never tasted a better stew."

"You can do it yourself," Justin said. "He'll be here in a minute to suggest a refill." And sure enough, at that moment, Cookie pushed through the swing doors from the kitchen. A big black kettle hung from one huge fist and, without asking, he refilled Hilary's bowl.

"Oh, my. I don't know..." she began.

Cookie scowled at her and she sighed. "Thank you. It's really delicious."

He nodded then and retreated to the kitchen. She looked up to find Justin smiling at her. "You've won his heart," he said softly. "But I feel duty bound to warn you."

"He won't come back with that kettle again, will he?" For a moment, caught up in their camaraderie, she forgot what had happened between them, forgot that she had to be on her guard.

Justin chuckled. "Not with the kettle. With chocolate layer cake." His eyes sparkled. "And if you don't eat it, he'll be offended." He chuckled again. "Deeply offended."

"Then I guess I'll just have to force it down."

For the first time in a long time she heard him laugh. The deep joyful sound of it vibrated through her, making her want to laugh, too. He reached across the table to touch her hand, just as he had in the old days when they'd laughed over some silliness or other. Realization hit her sharply and she jerked her hand away. "Do you have any questions about this morning?" she asked stiffly.

He looked disappointed, but he merely said, "Yes. Why did you make such a fuss about the mare and foal being stabled? I figured they'd be safer there."

Hilary shrugged. "I suppose you'd be safer in your bedroom. Would you like to stay there for two weeks?"

"Of course not. I'd go out of my mind. I guess I didn't look at it that way."

She ate for a few more minutes, striving to keep her attention on her food, reminding herself that Justin was just her boss. He could never be anything more. "Do you know what happened when your cowhand got kicked?"

He looked a little sheepish. "Not exactly. I was out of town on business. They told me..." He paused. "Pete told me the mare kicked his buddy, Joe. Broke his arm. Pete said the mare was a rogue, that she went after Joe. He didn't like her."

Hilary shook her head in exasperation. How could he be so dense? "So, today this hand who doesn't like the mare comes and takes away her foal."

"You're glaring at me again," Justin said, his dark eyes burning at her, reminding her of so many things, so many feelings. "I let him go early this morning. His buddy won't be coming back, either."

"Well, thank goodness for small favors," said Hilary, striving for a lightness she didn't feel.

A sound behind her made her turn her head and Cookie came in, pushing through the swing doors, carrying the two biggest pieces of chocolate layer cake she had ever seen. "Oh my! It's...it's beautiful."

"You eat it all," Cookie said, grinning at her. "You're skinny as a rail. Too bad she don't eat here, boss. I'd soon put some flesh on them bones."

"A good idea, Cookie." Justin beamed, his eyes avoiding the surprise in hers. "Miss Benson will have lunch here every day. You'll be in your glory feeding her."

"Oh, I can't. I . . ." She tried to make her protest stick, but the crestfallen look on the cook's face stopped her. What was the point in fighting them? She was going to be forced to accept Justin's company one way or another. "Oh, all right. For a while."

Four

The middle of the next morning found Hilary approaching the east pasture. Most of the men had gathered to watch. Some looked actually alarmed as she went over the fence. These men knew the damage a rogue could do. But Hilary had no qualms about the mare. Horses were not only intelligent and curious, as she had told Justin, they were also capable of gratitude. The mare would be her friend for life; there was no doubt in her mind about it.

In a way, she thought, the incident had been helpful. It immediately established her as a friend, a position it would ordinarily have taken her some time to reach. Ideally, she should have been handling the mare for weeks before the foaling, as she was planning to do with Justin's other mares that were soon to give birth.

As she neared the horse, she began humming quietly under her breath. Morning Glory raised her head and whuffled a greeting, her curious baby looking up from the grass he was pretending to nibble. Hilary laughed softly. She would have sworn she saw recognition and welcome in the foal's liquid brown eyes.

She set to work grooming the mare, admiring her coat, which was the color of peach fuzz. Many claybanks were yellower, hence their name. But Morning Glory was a lovely shade and it looked like Star would be about the same color as his mother. She didn't ignore the baby, but she didn't pay him so much attention that his mother felt concern. He came bouncing over on his long legs to watch. Hilary laughed at the expression of curiosity on his little face. She finished grooming the mare's left side and held out the brush to him. Little Star backed off a step and sniffed warily. Hilary chuckled. "Here little fellow. See? It won't hurt you."

She gave him time for a good long look before she drew it slowly and carefully over his small fuzzy side. He turned his head, looking back over his shoulder in surprise at the feeling of this strange thing. Laughing rose to Hilary's lips again. This was the best time of all the year. The foals were so cute, so playful.

She left off brushing him and moved to his mother's other side. Star was a bright little baby. It shouldn't take too long to bridge the gap in his training that had been caused by the delay after his birth. He gamboled off, paused a little distance away and looked at her, cocking his head. Hilary laughed appreciatively and a ripple of male laughter sounded from the crowd by the fence. Startled by the sound, the foal jumped, tangling his feet in the process and landing in an ungainly heap.

Hilary put down the brush and went to help him. "There you are," she said, lifting one little hoof and setting it straighter. "No need to worry, little fellow. They're just laughing cause you're so cute. Come on, let's go find Momma." Hand on his neck, she guided him back to Morning Glory and resumed her grooming.

She worked for more than an hour, grooming the grazing mare, letting the foal get to know her. Comfortable in the company of the horses, she almost forgot the men who were still watching. And then she looked up and saw that Justin was there.

She was tempted to stay longer with the horses to avoid talking to him. But she knew that would not be wise. She had established rapport with the mare, and the way her nerves were acting up now the mare and her foal were sure to sense it. No sense in complicating things. She gave them each a final pat, picked up the grooming implements and returned to the fence.

Avoiding Justin's eyes, she asked the assembled men, "Any questions?"

There was no reply.

"Good. The general idea is to be friends with the mare. She must accept you if you expect to get anywhere with the foal. I'm a little behind with Star because I lost those weeks after his birth. But he'll catch up. He's a bright little fellow."

She scrutinized the weather-beaten faces. "I know this way seems to take a long time, but, believe me, it's worth it."

"That's it for this morning. I think it's best if the rest of you leave Morning Glory and her foal alone for a while. She had a bad scare yesterday. I'd rather not remind her of it."

Heads nodded. She could see no resentment on their faces, only curiosity and some skepticism. But that skepticism would fade, she thought, once they saw her results.

"So the mare isn't a rogue," Justin said, his voice tingling down her spine.

She wanted to run, but she forced herself to turn and look at him. "Of course not. I told you that. She'll be fine as long as no one bothers her baby."

Justin nodded. "How's my filly?"

"She's doing fine. I put them out to pasture yesterday. Three days is the limit in the stable unless the weather turns bad."

"Will you work with her the same way?"

"Yes." He was wearing dirty scuffed boots, faded jeans and shirt, and a battered Stetson, but he looked handsome. "Actually, it's more like play. You exploit the foal's curiosity. You have to be careful not to push too much or too hard. To remember that he's only a baby."

She had a sudden swift vision of herself with a baby in her arms, a baby with Justin's dark hair and eyes. She swallowed hastily. "The mare mustn't get jealous, so you have to pay attention to her, too. The foal takes his feelings from her."

Justin nodded. "Yes, I gathered that." His eyes slid over her and her body grew warm. "See you at lunch," he said. "Keep up the good work."

For a moment after he left her, she just stood there, hurting. Would the pain never let up? she asked herself. Would it always hurt this much to see him? Time was supposed to heal all things, but it certainly took a lot of it.

The days passed. Late May turned into June. Hilary worked herself hard, arriving at the Rocking J every morning just after sunrise, returning home after a satisfying lunch. She finally convinced Cookie that two helpings of everything was all she could handle, and she ate his meals gratefully. For the first time in months, she was beginning to feel herself again.

Justin was not always there at noon. His business still demanded that he make frequent trips back East in his Lear jet. But, since he never knew exactly when this was going to be necessary, Cookie always made lunch.

Knowing this, and looking at Cookie's disappointed face the first time she tried to back out of it, Hilary had finally given in. Not only did it make it much easier to get straight to work once she reached home, it also enabled her to eat a light supper and save even more on the grocery bill.

The job seemed to be going well. The horses were responding to her training. Morning Glory had recovered from her fright and welcomed Hilary enthusiastically whenever she went to work with the foal. And Star was making great progress. She had never seen a livelier, more intelligent baby.

What hadn't changed was her feeling for Justin. No matter how she talked to herself, no matter how often she reminded herself of what Justin had done, she could not change the way she felt each time she saw him. It was stupid of her, she knew, to still want the man.

Why couldn't he have just stayed back East? she thought late one morning as she groomed another mare due to foal any day. She'd been happy with Papa. She paused, the brush suspended in midair. Well, maybe not exactly happy, not like she'd been with Justin. But she'd been contented. Things had been going well.

There had been none of the sharp aching sweetness that Justin brought into her life. But she really hadn't missed it. How could she have missed what she had never known and what she couldn't have begun to imagine?

The brush continued its downward stroke on the chestnut's gleaming flank, but Hilary's mind was elsewhere, back on the prairie that warm summer night. How good, how right, his body had felt against hers. How her breasts had quivered under his touch! Her whole body had come alive with feelings and reactions unlike anything she'd ever felt.

The prairie had seemed a fitting place. By mutual consent they drove out, away from Havre, into the seemingly endless grass, back to the little clump of cottonwoods that marked the bend in the small winding stream. Back to the spot where they had first seen each other.

The moon was almost full, silvering the tops of the buffalo grass and shimmering on the surface of the little stream, making the prairie into a wonderland, a fairy-tale place. Hand in hand they walked under the fluttering cottonwoods to the stream's edge.

No words passed between them as he took her in his arms, and his mouth devoured hers. She had experienced his kisses before, wild, savage possessions that drove the breath from her body and made her long for the consummation she had never known.

Her body fit itself naturally into his, her curving softness against his lean hard strength. She felt his desire pressing against her and she was filled with wild elation.

As though echoing her thoughts, his mouth left hers and moved to her ear. "My God, Hilary, I want you! I want you now."

"Justin, my love, I want you too." She had no false modesty, no sense of shame or uncertainty. Making love was a natural thing, what man and woman were made for. All her life she'd been waiting for Justin to say these very words. All her life she'd been waiting to join her aching body to his.

His hands were already at her buttons and hers joined them, together they worked feverishly to rid themselves of that last barrier between them, the flimsy layers of cloth that prevented their final intimacy. He paused only once in that passionate undressing to mumble between kisses, "I forgot to ask. Protection . . ."

She laughed softly, touched by his concern, her hands continuing their work. "I'm a rancher, darling. I know the facts of life. No need to worry."

No, they didn't worry. Nothing marred the perfection of their first coming together. She gasped as her bare flesh met his, as nerves she had never known she possessed flashed into brilliant life, as her body flamed with desire. His mouth insistent on hers, he pulled her down onto the prairie with him. She was vaguely aware of the crushed buffalo grass beneath her, of the whispering of cottonwood leaves overhead, but only momentarily. Then all her consciousness was focused on the strong male body that covered hers. Her flesh responded to his, fitting as closely against him as if they really were the two halves of one divided whole.

She clutched at him, her body moving of its own accord against his. There were no words to describe the glory that filled her whole being. Words were far too inadequate, she thought hazily. She was bathed in warm golden desire. Waves of joy rose deep, deep within her, lapping all her cells in warm heavenly bliss.

His mouth left hers and she reached for him blindly, not knowing where he was going until she felt his tongue on her naked breasts. Her flesh quivered as his mouth moved hungrily over her, as his hands roamed her eager body.

Something was building within her, growing and growing, something so beautiful, waiting to burst into being. "Please, please," she begged, hardly knowing what she said, knowing only that she desperately needed the consummation that was so near and yet kept eluding her. He moved over her then, his hard male body heavy on her, pushing her down into the prairie.

There was only one sharp twinge as he entered. She felt his hesitation and she grabbed at his shoulders, pulling him to her. "Please, please. Oh, Justin. Now, now!" The words poured from her. And then he was going on, thrusting against the aching body that arched up to meet his. And that something that was growing inside her flamed higher and higher until suddenly it burst like some great Roman candle, bathing her in a shower of warm golden sparks.

That night the ringing of the phone brought her instantly awake. "Yes," she replied to the hurried words of Justin's ranch hand. "Send a truck for me. I'll be ready." She would not have minded a moonlight ride across the prairie on Brandy. But if two of Justin's mares were foaling, there was no time for that. She had planned to be there for the chestnut anyway. She rubbed at her tired eyes. The foaling season would soon be over. Maybe then she could sleep the night through.

The mare's labor was pretty well along. Hilary took a look at her, before she moved along a few stalls to speak to the vet. "Hi, Vic. How's it going?"

Vic's face lit up. "Glad you're here, girl. This one's giving me a bit of trouble. Looks like you'll have to manage the chestnut yourself."

"No problem," she said, looking down at the restless mare he was soothing. "First time nerves?" she asked, hoping nothing else was wrong with Justin's mare.

Vic nodded. "Yeah. She's scared. But she'll make it. Looks like she's a veteran at this sort of thing."

Hilary nodded. "Even so, I'd better get back to her. Oh, where is Mr. Porter?"

Vic frowned. "I reckon he's away somewhere. One of those business trips he's always taking."

"Of course." Hilary made the words as non-committal as possible. She hurried back to her charge, not sure whether she was feeling relief or disappointment. On the way over, seated beside the silent ranch hand, she'd been thinking of the night of Golden Lady's birth. It was too bad Justin wouldn't be here to witness the miracle again. But it was probably better that he wasn't. She found it hard to concentrate on anything else when he was around.

She settled herself in the straw beside the mare's head, making the same, soothing noises that she usually made. Her hand moved automatically on the soft velvet nose, down the gleaming neck. What was it like, she mused, to have a baby? To carry within yourself a new life?

Hilary sighed. Before the wager, floating in the beauty of their love, she had built the most glowing daydreams; she and Justin looking down at their first born as it lay in her arms; she and Justin standing outside the corral, their arms around each other, watching the spring foals at play, while beside them stood their own children. Her childhood had been such a lonely one that long ago she had decided to have many children. There should always be someone there to play with, to be close to.

Hilary closed her eyes, blinking back the hot tears. She ought to forget those dreams. They wouldn't work without Justin. They were all built around him. There would be no dark-haired, dark-eyed babies to cuddle and coo at, because much as she still wanted him, she could never marry Justin Porter.

He hadn't been there when Papa was killed in the truck. But he'd been at the poker game that Papa was returning from, gambling and drinking with the rest of them.

The mare snorted as the foal's front legs and head appeared and Hilary spoke to her, soft, soothing words.

Hilary's eyelids were so heavy. Her arms and legs felt like lead. Last night she hadn't slept much. One of the Circle K mares had foaled and she'd spent most of the night with her, finishing just in time to wash up and come to work at the Rocking J. And tonight she'd only had about two hours sleep before the phone woke her again. From the looks of things this was going to be another all night job.

She managed a tired smile. Well, she told herself, this is what you wanted. You wanted to raise horses and horses are born at night. Inevitably.

It took most of the night. Vic finished about 3:00 a.m. and offered to relieve her, but Hilary sent him on his way. He had more than enough to do.

By four Sunrise's new foal was on its feet nursing and by four-thirty the afterbirth had come, and been set aside for Vic's inspection when he returned the next day.

Heaving a sigh, Hilary looked around the silent stable. There was no point in rousing a hand to drive her home now. In only a few hours she would have to be back at work.

She left the mare and foal in the stall, engrossed in each other, and made for the tack room and an old horse blanket she'd noticed there. Five minutes later she was stretched out on the floor outside the mare's stall, her head pillowed on her battered hat, the horse blanket pulled up around her neck. The fragrant smell of straw and hay mingled with the comforting smell of horses. Taking a deep breath, Hilary let herself go deep into sleep.

She dreamed of Justin, of course. His brown eyes mocked her, and his heavy dark brows drew together as he taunted her. "Horses? You don't know the first thing about horses."

"I do, I do." She argued with him, pleaded with him. But he was adamant.

"No, you can't train my horses. I don't want you around."

It seared her soul, the pain of those awful words. Tears poured from her eyes and ran down her cheeks. "Why, Justin, why?"

But for all her pleading, Justin gave her no answers. "I love you, Justin," she murmured, tossing restlessly under the blanket. "I need you."

The stable was dim, but it was surprise not darkness that stopped the big man just inside the door. For a moment he thought he was going mad, wanting her so much that he had started hearing her voice. But as he moved closer, he saw her. The blanket had been tossed aside by her restless turnings. Tears glistened on her cheeks, and under her faded shirt her breasts rose and fell with the force of her feelings.

"Please, Justin." The words were mumbled, but he made them out. "I love you. Don't leave me."

She's dreaming, he thought, a tender smile softening the hard lines of his face. She's dreaming of me.

"Justin!" The word was a long wail of anguish. Hearing it, he didn't think; he just acted. The next thing he knew he was down there in the straw beside her, gathering her close in his arms. "It's all right, honey. It's all right. I'm here."

He kissed the tears from her face and smoothed the tousled hair back from her forehead with trembling fingers. It had been so long since he'd been able to touch her.

A smile pulled at the corners of her mouth as she snuggled against him. "Oh, Justin. I love you."

It was just too much for him. He knew she was dreaming, knew she had no idea of what she was saying or that he was really there, holding her in his arms. But he couldn't help himself. His mouth covered hers, and his arms clasped her to his aching body.

It was like a miracle, he thought, as the lips under his parted and returned his kiss. She did still love him. She must, to behave like this. Exhilaration coursed through him. She did love him.

Deep in her dream, Hilary felt the comfort of a warm male body. He was holding her. Justin was holding her. She relaxed against him. This was the Justin she knew so well. The kind, loving man who was there when she needed him.

He kissed her then, a kiss so real that her own mouth responded and she burrowed closer against him. Awareness hovered on the edge of her consciousness. She knew that she was dreaming. In the world of dreams she was giving herself what in the real world she couldn't have. It was only a dream, so it was all right.

But then, as his kiss grew more persuasive, as his tongue took possession of her mouth, consciousness intruded into her pleasant dream. This was real, too real.

Almost against her will, she fought her way back to consciousness and opened her eyes. His face was only inches from hers, his dark eyes full of tenderness. She blinked. Was she still dreaming?

"Wh-what?" She tried to sit up and realized that he was cradling her in his arms. Hastily, she pulled away. "What are you doing here?"

"I just got home and came out to check on the mares. You were having a nightmare. You called out."

"What did I say?" Color flooded her cheeks as the details of the dream came back to her. She distinctly remembered pleading with Justin not to leave her, telling him that she loved him.

He sat back on his heels, his face in the shadows. "I couldn't make it out." He wasn't sure why he lied; he only knew he couldn't force her to admit to loving him. But at least now he knew it was true; he knew that she did love him. "You screamed once. You seemed awfully scared. So I tried to wake you."

"I see." She was very tired and though parts of the dream seemed crystal clear, she had no recollection of screaming. Her lips still burned with the passion of that kiss. She licked them nervously. That must have been part of the dream. God knew, it wouldn't be the first time she'd dreamed of his kisses. And probably not the last.

"Why are you sleeping out here?" he asked, looking around them.

"Jessie's Belle foaled last night. So did Sunrise. Vic couldn't handle them both so someone came for me. By the time she was done it was almost dawn. It seemed foolish to wake someone to take me home. So I decided to grab a few winks here."

"You could have gone up to the house," he said in exasperation. "There *are* extra beds there."

She shrugged. "It just didn't occur to me. It's not the first night I've spent in a stable." Tired as she was, she managed a little smile. "The beds aren't too soft, but the company's good."

Realizing suddenly that beds were not a safe topic of conversation for them, she reached for her hat. "I guess I might as well get to work. It'll be sunup soon."

"You'll do no such thing." He kept his voice low, but it carried the weight of authority. "You're going to come up to the house with me and sleep."

"I don't need to..." she began, wishing he would move farther away. That distinctive male scent of his was playing havoc with her tired senses.

"You might know a lot about horses," Justin said briskly, "but you're woefully ignorant of the human body. You can't keep going without sleep like this. Your mares are still foaling, too, aren't they?"

"Yes." She was so tired her head was swimming. She couldn't seem to keep her eyes focused properly.

"How long since you've slept a night through?" he demanded.

She was too tired to lie. "I don't remember exactly. Maybe a week or so."

Justin got to his feet and stood towering over her. She struggled to get to her own, but had to stop at her knees, where she remained, swaying slightly from the effort. "I'll just doze awhile here, then."

"You'll do no such thing," he said gruffly. "You're going to bed. And you're going now."

"You can't tell me what to..." she began, searching for some anger to fight him with, trying not to think of how exhausted she really was. But before she could make her tired brain work, he had lifted her into his arms and was striding toward the door.

"Justin! Put me down." She struggled in his arms.

"Be quiet," he said sternly. "You'll panic the mares and you know that's not good for them."

She subsided then. Tired as she was, there was no way she could make him stop and put her down. She was too weary to fight, too weary even to think.

But not too weary to feel, she realized as the stable door swung shut behind them. The sun was just coming up, pale fingers of golden light streaking the eastern sky. Hilary sighed. Dawn was her favorite time of day. Everything seemed fresh and new then, time for a new beginning.

She swallowed hastily over the lump in her throat and closed her eyes. There would be no new beginning for her and Justin. What he had done was unforgivable. The facts were clear. Papa had been all right until that wager with Justin.

She tried to remember this as Justin carried her across the ranch yard. He was strong. Even as skinny as she'd become these past months, she was no light load. But he strode along as though her weight was nothing to him. He was a big man. That was one of the reasons she'd been attracted to him. Beside him she felt small and feminine. Vulnerable in a wonderful way.

But she must not be vulnerable, she thought, as her mind whirled, and her senses were swamped with the smell, and feel of him. His distinctive scent, so clean and fresh, so masculine and virile, made her feel even more light-headed. Against her cheek she felt the fabric of his suit coat, but even more, she felt the beating of his heart.

She longed to lie there forever, close against his strong heart. Her own heart pounded heavily as she recalled that dream kiss. Had it really been a dream? It had seemed so real. He'd been holding her in his arms when she woke. He could have been kissing her, too. But there was no way to find out. She certainly couldn't ask him, couldn't reveal that she'd been dreaming about *him*, about him kissing her. It must have been a dream.

He had reached the house now and was striding up the stairs and into one of the spare rooms. He deposited her roughly on the bed. "Now," he said, glaring down at her. "You're going to sleep until noon."

"But I have work. The horses . . ."

"The horses will just have to wait," he said gruffly. "They can miss one day's workout. I'll send someone to wake you in time for lunch." His eyes burned down at her. "And I give you fair warning, Hilary Benson. If I find you out of this bed before then, I'll carry you up here again. In front of all the hands. And *that* is a promise. Now sleep."

He reached down and pulled off her boots then, spread the blanket carefully over her. "Good night."

She was already half asleep, too tired to even think of defying him. She mumbled, "Yes, boss," in what she hoped was a sarcastic tone, and then curling up on her side, she let sleep claim her.

Five

———

Meeting Cookie on her way to lunch, Hilary managed a smile. She felt a hundred percent better. Justin was right in what he'd said. The human body could only handle so much and she had not been taking very good care of hers lately. Keeping the ranch going had taken all her efforts and she had skimped on her meals. After Papa's death she'd lost her appetite and it had been easy not to eat much, especially with money so short. But now Cookie's lunches were perking her up. She was even getting hungry at suppertime. And, thanks to the arrival of her salary check, the pantry shelves were no longer bare.

It was time, she told herself firmly, to look after Hilary Benson. If she got sick, there would be no one to take care of the horses, no one to give them the training they needed. Jeb could never do it all alone.

Justin strode into the dining room and slid into his seat. His Stetson was dusty and his shirt and jeans were in no better shape. She found herself wishing she'd been out on the range with him.

"So," he said, looking her over so carefully that she felt the warmth flooding her body. "How did you sleep?"

"Like a log," she replied, forcing herself to meet his gaze. If he had really kissed her like that, if it hadn't been a dream, something in his expression might give him away. But his face revealed nothing. He looked just as he usually did these days— brisk and businesslike.

"You've been working too hard," he said sternly. "You . . ."

"I know," she replied meekly, so meekly that his mouth dropped open and he stared at her.

"You know?" he said, echoing her words.

"Yes, I know." She ran her hand through the tangle of her hair. "Foaling season will be over before too long. Things will settle down some then. I'll be able to sleep every night."

He nodded. "That might help."

"From the way you're talking, I'm beginning to think I must look pretty awful." She meant the words to lighten the atmosphere, but the look he gave her left her with legs so weak she was glad to be sitting down.

"No," he said, in that soft intimate tone she hadn't heard for so long. "No, you look as beautiful as ever."

She knew she should pull her eyes away from his. But somehow she couldn't. His thoughts lay open to her. In his burning gaze she could read desire and longing.

Her nails dug into her palms as she struggled not to respond to the appeal in his eyes, struggled not to give in to the waves of tenderness that she was feeling.

The swing doors opened and Cookie came in, bearing bowls of chili and a platter of crusty bread. Hilary wrenched her eyes away from Justin and smiled at the big cook. "Yum. My favorite."

Cookie was unconvinced. "You say that about everything I make, Miss Hilary."

She shook her head. "I can't help it, Cookie. It's true. Everything you serve tastes so good."

Cookie's grin broadened. "Bet I know your favorite dessert, though."

Hilary threw up her hands in surrender. "You've guessed my deepest secret, Cookie. I'm addicted to chocolate."

Cookie's laughter boomed. "Don't I know it, miss. The way you go after my chocolate layer cake..." He shook his head. "I'm gonna bake you one this very afternoon."

"Better wait until tomorrow," Justin said.

Both Hilary and Cookie turned to him in surprise.

"I was about to tell you," Justin went on. "You'll need a change of clothes in the morning. We're flying to Kentucky."

"Flying? Kentucky?" She didn't understand.

"Yes." A glance sent Cookie back to the kitchen. "We're going to look at some new stock. The Harrison Farm near Lexington has some mares for sale. A stallion, too."

"You can do that alone," Hilary protested. "I can't leave here. The mares and foals need me. My place..." Her words faltered to a stop under the scrutiny of his eyes.

"Vic can take care of the mares. Jeb can handle your place for one day. We won't be gone that long."

"I—"

"I need your help on this, Hilary." His dark eyes threatened to pull her into their depths. "I know I don't really have the right to ask it of you, but..."

If he had insisted that she go, she would have immediately refused. But since he had asked for her help... And she *was* his trainer. The new mares and stallion would be under her care. It made sense for her to be there, to have a say in choosing them.

He was still looking at her, his spoon poised over his bowl, a frown wrinkling his dark forehead.

She gave in. Common sense was on his side. "Well, okay. I guess it'll be all right."

"Thank you."

The relief in his eyes seemed a little out of proportion. It was just a trip to look at new stock. If he thought it was going to be more . . . She pushed the idea away. That stupid dream was affecting her judgment.

The next morning as she approached his landing strip in the truck Justin had sent to pick her up, she was already regretting her decision. She had let that pleading look of his get to her. And now she was going away with him. The memory of that dream kiss was haunting her. There was something different about the way he treated her now, something she couldn't put her finger on.

He was waiting by the plane. "Good morning," he said as he took her shoulder bag. "Is this all?"

She nodded. "I travel light."

"So I see. Well, we're ready." He turned to the waiting hand. "You've got my instructions . . ."

"Yeah, boss. Good luck."

The interior of the plane was more functional than luxurious, but still Hilary felt strange entering it. It had taken her a long while to get used to his money, to the fact that he kept his own private plane at a landing strip near the ranch house. She took her place in the seat next to his.

"Ready?" Justin asked.

"Yes." She forced herself to relax. She was not as used to flying as he was. It was nothing to him—like driving a car. She shut her eyes and leaned back in the seat.

"Still scared of flying?" he asked.

She refused to open her eyes. There was no use in trying to lie to him. He knew everything about her. "Yes," she said. "But I can handle it."

"I know that. I doubt if there's anything you can't handle."

There was something about his tone. She opened her eyes slightly and turned her head to look at his profile outlined against the blue of the Montana sky. He was busy with the plane, and she allowed herself the luxury of a long look. His nose was bold, but not too large for his face. From this angle, she could only see one of his dark brows, but she could remember how they met in the middle of his forehead when he was upset over something. And his chin... Her fingers tingled with the remembered feel of it. Smooth after shaving. Rough with dark whiskers when he woke beside her in the morning.

She clasped her hands tightly together in her lap. She had to stop this kind of thing. She would get over Justin. It was just taking a little longer than she'd thought it would.

She closed her eyes, but his image lingered there in the darkness under her eyelids. She swallowed a silent sob. How was she ever going to forget what he had been to her when by his presence he was always reminding her of the joy they had once shared?

"Hilary." His hand was warm on her shoulder. "Hilary. Wake up."

She opened her eyes slowly, reluctant to leave the safe world of sleep.

"We're there?" she asked, realizing that he was out of his seat. She pushed herself erect. "We're there already?"

"Yes," he replied. "Already. Did you by any chance attend another foaling last night?"

"No." She rubbed at her eyes. "I ... Because I slept so late yesterday I had trouble getting to sleep last night." No need to tell him that she'd been thinking about him, him and that kiss. The more she thought about that dream kiss the more confused she became. Was it a dream? Or was it real? And the most irritating thing of all was that she had absolutely no way to find out.

"Here comes Harrison," Justin said. "Remember our signals?"

Hilary nodded. When they'd first started shopping for his horses, they'd created a series of signals to communicate with each other. It simplified matters a great deal—and it helped him know what she thought about an animal without revealing anything to the owner.

Peter Harrison was approaching fifty. He was still lean and fit, his sandy hair only showing a smattering of gray. He extended a tanned hand. "Good to meet you, Mr. Porter," he said, extending a hand.

"Justin. And this is my trainer, Hilary Benson."

Hilary took the outstretched hand. "Pleased to meet you, Mr. Harrison." She liked the man already. His handshake was good and firm.

"Let's make it first names all around," Peter Harrison suggested. "Unless Miss Benson objects."

"Not at all, Peter." She returned the man's smile.

Harrison gestured. "The Jeep's right over there. Would you like to go up to the house first and freshen up?"

Hilary would have much preferred to go directly to the horses, but Justin nodded. "Thank you, Peter. That's very kind of you. I could use a quick shower. The flight took a little more out of me than I expected."

"Of course." Peter motioned them into the Jeep. "No rush. We have plenty of time."

The house, as Peter Harrison called it, was a huge white mansion, and looked to Hilary's eyes more like a hotel. She took the hand that he offered her and climbed nimbly out of the Jeep. "This way," he said. "My wife'll be glad to see you." He grinned at Hilary. "She's always complaining that so many of our guests are men. She likes a good gossip now and then.''

Hilary smiled, wondering how much she would have in common with this man's wife. "Then I'm afraid I won't be much use to her," she said. "The only thing I know about is horses."

Harrison chuckled. "It doesn't matter. She'll still be glad to see you."

As though to confirm this, a door opened onto the veranda. "Here she comes now." He turned to greet the approaching woman with a smile.

To her surprise, Hilary saw a woman close to her own age. In faded jeans and shirt, and with a stained apron tied round her waist, Marian Harrison looked more like a housekeeper than the wife of a wealthy Kentuckian.

She wiped at her cheek with the back of her hand, leaving a streak of flour there. "Hello," she said. "Sorry to greet you like this."

"It's quite all right," Justin said, turning on the smile that was guaranteed to charm anything female. "Pleased to meet you."

"So you're Justin Porter." Marian Harrison's eyes were frankly appraising and bubbling with gaiety. "Well, I must say you live up to your reputation."

Hilary found herself laughing at the startled expression on Justin's face.

"My reputation?" he repeated.

Peter Harrison laughed softly. "I'm afraid my wife's been listening to gossip. She knows someone who knows someone who knows you."

"Oh." Somewhat to Hilary's surprise, Justin didn't show any interest whatsoever in the identity of this someone. He looked at Harrison. "The place to freshen up?" he suggested.

"Of course." Marian Harrison became the perfect hostess. "Your rooms are this way."

"Rooms, I thought—"

The pressure of Justin's fingers on her elbow surprised Hilary into silence. There was some reason he wanted her to accept this. With his fingers burning into her flesh she couldn't help wondering if that reason really had anything to do with horses. Still, he *was* her boss and they *were* on a buying trip.

They followed their hostess up a staircase that rivaled something from *Gone with the Wind*. "Here," she said. "I've put you next to each other." She smiled briefly. "And now I'll leave you to your freshening up. There's a cold buffet in the breakfast room. Sorry, I've got to run. We're having twenty for dinner and I'm making my special Kentucky cake. See you later."

Hilary watched her walk away. Twenty for dinner, she thought, shaking her head. And making dessert herself.

Justin chuckled. "Don't look so surprised. Wealthy women can enjoy cooking."

"So I see." She turned toward her room.

"Half an hour?" Justin said. "We might as well eat before we start looking. They say it's not good to shop on an empty stomach."

She chuckled at his little joke, trying not to remember how it had once been, how they had laughed at everything, laughed together. "I think that's food shopping you're talking about, not horses. But at any rate, I'll be ready."

The room, she thought, as she closed the door softly behind her, was like something out of a movie. It would make three or four of her bedroom at home. A white brick fireplace graced the outside wall, flanked by curtain-ruffled French doors that led out onto a broad upstairs porch overlooking a garden rich in blooming flowers.

Some of those same flowers filled the vases that were scattered throughout the room, scenting the air with their sweet fragrance. The furniture was antique white, touched with gold. A giant canopy bed, with ruffled peach spread and curtains, was matched by two huge dressers and an old-fashioned full-length mirror on a stand. In one corner stood a chaise lounge covered in chocolate-brown velvet. Beside it, a small white table held a ruffled reading lamp, one of the latest novels and, incredibly, a box of chocolates.

Still clutching her shoulder bag, afraid to put it down on the white shag carpet, Hilary advanced carefully across the room to the door that must open to a private bath.

She stood in the doorway, her breath deserting her in one long whoosh. This bathroom put even the bedroom to shame. All gleaming white tile and brass fixtures, it looked like something out of the *Arabian Nights*. Hilary took another step and gasped. It was really there, an honest-to-goodness sunken bathtub. And on a glass shelf along the wall stood an array of bottles and a little sign that said For Your Bathing Pleasure.

She dropped the bag on the chocolate-colored carpet and knelt by the tub. Each bottle, she saw on closer inspection, was labeled. She chose one that said Garden Fragrance and started to run the water.

This place was stupendous, she thought, getting to her feet. Half an hour wasn't going to be nearly long enough. She could soak in that tub for hours and hours. Stripping off her clothes, she turned back to the long white and brass vanity that held not one, but two sinks. In one corner stood a pile of thick fluffy white towels and in the other a hair dryer, a new shower cap and a package of bobby pins. Hilary shook her head. Everything possible had been provided for the comfort of a guest. She smiled to herself as she sank into the warm, bubble-filled tub. So this was how the wealthy lived.

Half an hour later, feeling incredibly refreshed, she stepped out into the hall to meet Justin. "This is how you buy horses?" she asked, raising an eyebrow. She was thankful that Justin was still wearing ranch clothes. She had changed into her clean jeans and shirt. There was no more she could do.

Justin sniffed. "Something smells good."

She felt the warmth building inside her. Would he never stop affecting her this way? "Bubble bath. This place has everything."

"Smells like flowers, prairie flowers." His eyes were dark with desire. Had his remark about prairie flowers been meant to remind her of their first night together? Damn that stupid dream. It was distorting all her perceptions. "Do you think we can find the breakfast room before dinnertime?" she asked, hoping to dispel her feelings with a little humor.

His eyes twinkled and his lips curved into a smile. "Trust me. I have a wonderful sense of direction."

"I hope so," she said, wishing she could laugh with him, laugh without remembering how it had once been. "I have a horrendous appetite now. Cookie has spoiled me. I've become like a dog. At mealtime my stomach automatically activates."

"Mine, too," Justin said. "So let's quit talking and eat."

After the cold buffet, which to Hilary had looked more like a banquet, Peter Harrison took them out to look at the horses.

"Are you interested in any particular color?" Peter asked.

Hilary shook her head. "Color's not so important. We're breeding for other qualities. Speed. Bottom. Intelligence. The sort of thing that makes a good quarter horse." She smiled at Harrison. "Are many people back here raising quarter horses now? I sort of associate Kentucky with thoroughbred racing, the Derby, that sort of thing."

Peter nodded. "You have the right idea, but a lot of people are getting into quarter horses now. The breed is popular as trail horses and show animals." He laughed. "You know its good qualities as well as I do. There's been a good bit of quarter horse racing, too. But, come on and see what we've got." He gestured toward the first paddock. "I think you'll agree there are some real beauties out here."

As they stepped up to the fence, Hilary drew a deep breath. The bluegrass of Kentucky seemed to set off the beauty of the grazing horses.

"The slate over there," Harrison said. "With the white blaze. The sorrel with white stockings to your left. The apricot dun under the tree."

"How about the seal brown over there?" Hilary asked. "And the medicine-hat paint?"

Peter Harrison laughed. "You've got yourself a real gem here, Justin. She's just picked out the two best-looking mares in the lot."

"Are they for sale?" Justin asked.

"Well, I might let the seal brown go. The medicine-hat paint is Marian's pet. She won't part with her, I know. She favors horses with paint markings. These are all first-year mares," he continued. "Ready for breeding. They'll give you strong, healthy foals."

Justin nodded. His eyes glided over the young mares, examining them, then came back to Hilary's. At her "yes" signal, he turned back to their host. "Okay, let's take a look at the stallion."

Harrison nodded. "He's several paddocks over. His stud book's in the tack room."

Hilary nodded. She had heard good things of this stallion's sire. And his dam had great blood lines, too. Betsy's Barracuda had made quite a name for himself. She looked forward to seeing him.

As they reached the paddock gate, she drew in another breath. She had never seen a lilac dun before and this one was magnificent. His dove-gray coat glistened in the sunlight as he reared and turned to inspect these intruders into his domain.

"He knows he's something," Hilary said softly. "And he's proud of it."

Harrison nodded.

"Why are you selling him?" Justin asked.

Harrison looked a little uncomfortable. "He's, ah, picked up some bad habits," he said finally. "Some owners might not tell you, but well, I prefer to be honest."

"What bad habits?" Hilary asked, her eyes never leaving the beautiful stallion.

"He, ah, likes to nip at your, ah, back pocket."

Hilary's laughter startled both men and they turned to look at her while out in the pasture the stallion's dark ears flicked in their direction.

"Does he have any other vices?" she asked, enjoying their surprise.

"He cribs sometimes," Harrison admitted.

"Anything else?"

He shook his head. "Isn't that enough?" he asked plaintively.

Hilary smiled sympathetically. "How long have you had him?"

"Just a year. His former owner neglected to tell me about these vices, as you call them. My trainers don't like such things." He turned to face them. "Frankly, we have a big operation here. I like to have it run smoothly. I can't afford to keep a horse that disrupts the routine."

He looked at Hilary. "I've been hearing things about you and your unorthodox methods. Good things." He grinned. "You wouldn't like a new job, would you?"

"Afraid not," Hilary said, her heart leaping as she noticed the look of fear that momentarily crossed Justin's face. "I've got a spread of my own back in Montana. And a few horses." Her eyes returned to the stallion, who was now cantering across the field, his long, chocolate-brown mane and tail flowing out behind him.

She did not consciously analyze a horse. At least, not at first. At first she relied on her gut feeling.

Only if it warned her that something was wrong did she look to see what that something might be.

But there was nothing wrong with this beauty that a little time and patience couldn't cure. He had beautiful conformation and his stud record was excellent. Probably he'd taken to cribbing out of boredom. They could easily cover up the wood in his stall so he couldn't chew it. And when he had to be kept in, a volley ball on the floor would give him something else to do instead.

As for his habit of nipping back pockets, as Peter had so delicately put it, that could be just playfulness. With his unusual coloring he had probably received a lot of attention when a baby. Quite possibly some trainer had started this game and the stallion was only continuing what he had learned. And, thought Hilary with a secret smile, what he had once learned, he could unlearn. With time and patience. And for this beauty, she had plenty of both. She gave Justin the buy signal and held back her laughter at his look of surprise.

"How do you call him?" she asked. "Why hasn't he come over to visit with us?"

Harrison frowned. "The last trainer he nipped lost his temper and clouted him one. He's been a little shy since then."

Hilary nodded. "I see."

Harrison turned to include Justin in the conversation. "I know it takes awhile to decide about these things." He glanced at his watch. "Why don't you take your time? Look around. In fact, why don't you plan on staying the night? Marian would love that. You can join our guests for dinner and dancing.''

"I . . ." In her panic, Hilary forgot herself and tugged at Justin's sleeve. "I can't do that. I haven't any clothes."

Harrison smiled. "Not to worry. We keep a whole closet of evening dresses. There's bound to be something to fit you. Tell me your size and Marian will have some transferred to your closet."

"Ten," Hilary stammered. A closetful of clothes just for guests?

"And your shoe size?"

"Eight and a half."

"Good." His eyes twinkled. "You'll find other necessities there, too."

Stunned at this information, Hilary managed to mutter a thank-you.

"Well, I'll be getting back to the house. See you later. Dinner's at eight."

When he was out of earshot, Hilary turned accusingly to Justin. "I didn't bargain for this. You said we'd only be one day. Jeb will—"

"You can call Jeb and tell him we'll be home tomorrow. Haven't you told me many times not to buy on the spur of the moment?"

Hilary nodded.

He smiled. "So relax and enjoy yourself. I can see you're taken by the stallion, vices and all. I could have guessed, knowing your way with rogues. Do you really think you can cure him?''

"I'm not sure yet.'' Hilary looked again toward the stallion, away from Justin's face. "Why don't you leave me alone with him for a while? Since you're so determined to stay over, I might as well do something useful.''

Justin looked doubtful, a frown threatening to bring his dark brows together. "I don't like having you mess around with strange horses. You could get hurt.''

She had to laugh; she couldn't help it. "Me! Get hurt by a *horse*? Come on, Justin. Be serious.''

"I . . .'' She saw that muscle in his jaw tightening again. Then he sighed. "I guess there's no use in trying to get a promise out of you. To stay away from *him*?'' He gestured toward the field and the stallion, who now stood surveying them from a safe distance.

She nodded. "You're right. There's no use. Go on now. I'll be fine.''

He still looked skeptical, but he left, finally, shaking his head, to go back and take another look at the mares. Hilary waited until he was out of sight. Then, whistling a merry tune, she climbed the fence that stood between her and the waiting stallion.

Six

When she returned to the house several hours later, Hilary was smiling happily. Betsy's Barracuda was going to be a wonderful addition to the Rocking J's herd. And it wasn't going to be hard to cure him of his vices, not at all.

When she opened the door to her room, she thought she had prepared herself for anything, but she discovered differently. The closet door stood open and in it hung, not one but three long gowns, each of them in a shade to complement her coloring. Spread out on the bed she found a flimsy bra and panties, a long slip and panty hose. All in their original wrappers.

Hurrying into the bathroom, she quickly washed her hands, noticing as she did so that the vanity now held an assortment of cosmetics and several bottles of perfume.

Hilary shook her head. It was incredible to think that people actually lived like this.

She moved back into the bedroom, anxious to look at the gowns. They were all beautiful, but she knew the moment she saw it which one she would choose. A deep emerald green with a draped bodice and long flowing sleeves, the gown would cling tightly to her waist and flare out over her hips.

For a moment all thoughts of horses disappeared from her mind. She was woman, all woman, as she imagined herself in that gown.

Shaking her head, she turned back to the bathroom where she started the water running into the tub and poured in more Garden Fragrance. Its pleasant scent filled the room as she pulled off her boots. She frowned as she looked down at them. She'd been tempted to pull them off outside the door to the house, but the prospect of being found running around this palace in her stockinged feet was too much for her.

She stripped off the rest of her clothes and slipped into the warm water. The tub was built with just the right slant; she leaned back and sighed luxuriously. What would it be like to live like this?

You'd be bored silly in a week, she told herself. Just like one of your stabled horses. Nobody needs this much luxury. Besides, you wouldn't want to give up working with the foals. Face it, you'd never make a lady of leisure. And you would certainly never be able to content yourself with making dessert for guests.

She admitted that to herself. Still it was nice to relax once in a while. And as long as she had to stay here, she might as well enjoy it.

When she got out of the tub, finally, she wrapped herself in one of the huge fluffy towels and went back to the bedroom. It was still some time until dinner, but she was feeling the effects of a long day. Though they had gained two hours of clock time in the flight and though she had slept, it was not a restful sleep—and some of it had been feigned to keep from having to talk to Justin.

Carefully moving the lingerie to one side of the big bed, she pulled back the covers on the other and stretched out. She would just close her eyes for a little while.

When she opened them again, it was time to dress. She sat before the well-appointed vanity in the lacy underwear and brushed her hair until it shone in the soft light. Such a beautiful room. Such beautiful things. It was almost as though she'd been transported to another world.

The thought sobered her and her hand paused halfway to her scalp. This *was* another world, the world of the rich and affluent. And soon she was going to be part of it, meet twenty strangers.

She stared at herself in the mirror, then her hand continued its downward stroke. "No cold feet, Hilary Benson," she told her reflection sharply. "These are people just like any other people. Even if they do have loads of money."

She thought the same thing some time later as she opened the door and stepped out into the hall, moving carefully in the high-heeled sandals. The dress fit perfectly, clinging just where it should. Her hair flowed down her back in long, red-brown waves. She felt like someone else. Not like the Hilary Benson who every morning climbed into faded jeans and shirt, pulled on scuffed boots and set off to work with the horses.

She knocked softly on Justin's door, just as she had when she'd come in from the pasture, but there was no answer. Glancing at her watch, she shook her head. He must have already gone downstairs. She took a deep breath and steadied herself, then started after him.

At the foot of the stairs she paused, unsure of which way to go. But the sound of laughter floating in from outside led her in that direction. She paused at the French doors that led out onto a patio and the fragrant garden. The guests were gathered in little groups, chatting together. She breathed a silent prayer of thanks for Marian Harrison's wonderful closet. She could never have faced this group wearing jeans.

"There you are," cried Marian, coming toward her. "The dress fits perfectly."

"Yes, it does." Hilary managed a smile. "Thank you so much for loaning it to me. And the shoes."

"It's nothing." Marian shrugged. "Come on and meet our guests. Justin is off somewhere, talking horses, no doubt. But he'll be back."

For the next ten minutes, Hilary was busy trying to remember names and faces to go with them. And then Marian said, "And this is P. Taylor Morris. He's into horses, too. Oh, excuse me. I see that the cook needs me."

Hilary looked down at the drink she'd been given. At least Marian had dumped her on someone she could talk to, someone who knew horses.

She turned to the man beside her. He was a very big man, bigger even than Justin. She felt the little thrill that looking way up to a man always gave her. She so seldom met a man this much taller than she was. "Well, Mr. Morris, what kind of horses do you raise?"

"Race horses," he said, smiling at her from a pair of startlingly blue eyes and running a hand through his sun-bleached hair. He was probably close to forty, and very attractive.

"Really?" Hilary smiled up at him. This man was going to be interesting.

"Really," he said. "Please call me Taylor." His grin was infectious. "The *P* stands for a horrible ancestral name that I'm trying to forget."

"I see." She laughed along with him. "Well, Taylor, you must call me Hilary then."

His smile was warm. "That," he said softly, "was the whole idea." His hand brushed hers. "Can I freshen your drink? Get you a canapé? Do anything to put you eternally in my debt?"

She laughed. "No, thanks, I'm fine now." It was a pleasure to be with a man like this. She could enjoy his company without any of the terrible conflicting feelings that Justin raised.

"So you're from Montana," Taylor said. "Do you like it there?"

Hilary smiled. "You mean because of all the snow in the winter?"

His smile was really sweet, she thought as he nodded. "There is a lot of cold and snow," she agreed. "But we have lots of sunshine, too. That's one of the nicest things."

"Lots of sunshine?" Taylor repeated.

"Yes, all winter long. But then, I hardly know what it's like anywhere else. Though I did spend several winters in Texas."

"Let me guess," he said. "I bet you were in school there. Texas A&M?"

"Right the first time," Hilary replied. "Horse management. But where do you spend your winters?"

"Warm places," Taylor said, pretending to shiver. "Florida. California. The Bahamas. The Riviera."

Hilary chuckled. "That must be nice."

Taylor's face sobered. "It used to. It's kind of lonely now. Since I lost Mary Lou."

Hilary raised a questioning eyebrow.

"My wife," he said. "She died the winter before last."

"I'm so sorry," Hilary replied, as, without thinking she took his hand in hers.

"Thank you." His low voice conveyed his appreciation of her sympathy. "It took awhile, but I'm getting over it."

His fingers closed around her hand and with a start she withdrew it. "I lost my father about seven months ago. It was very hard."

"Yes." He put a comforting hand on her arm. "But you *will* get over it."

Sensing her discomfort with the subject, he smiled. "And that's enough sad talk. Let's make a pact. The rest of the evening will be fun. Agreed?"

"Agreed," replied Hilary, managing a smile to match his.

"Good. Then the first order of business is to get us another drink."

"No, thank you," Hilary said. "This one is fine." It was, in fact, untasted. She did from time to time raise the glass to her lips, but nothing actually reached them. She did not drink. Some people said it could be hereditary, the tendency toward alcoholism. And she had long ago decided that it would be wisest to live without the stuff.

"So," she said, "do you love horses or is it just a business with you?"

"What do you think?" His eyes were frankly admiring and she felt herself glowing as she basked in his appreciation of her as a woman.

"Well, let me have a look at you." He didn't shift his eyes or shuffle his feet; he seemed entirely unconcerned as she looked him over. "Your tan tells me you like the outdoors. But you could have gotten it in any of those warm places you were telling me about. The same for the sun lines around your eyes." Her gaze fell to his long legs. "And I can't see your legs to tell if they're bowed."

His laughter was hearty. It was good to laugh again, she thought, as she joined him. Good to have fun.

"My legs are not bowed," he assured her when they had stopped laughing. "I can promise you that." He took one of her hands in his. "Perhaps you'd like to feel my hands to see if they're work-callused."

They were not, as she already knew. She shook her head. "There aren't enough visible clues. Have you seen Barracuda?"

"Harrison's lilac dun? Of course. He's a beautiful beast. Quarter horses don't have the staying power of my thoroughbreds, but they can be beautiful animals."

Hilary smiled. "Okay. I know now. You do love horses."

Those blue eyes of his twinkled. "Really? And how do you know that?"

"I saw it in your eyes. And heard it in your voice," she replied smugly. "And you've obviously taken the time to look at Barracuda, though you have no business interest in him."

"I see. Well, Hilary, my dear, perhaps you ought to go into the detective business. You have marvelous powers of deduction."

She laughed softly. "I'm afraid they only work where horses are concerned."

His eyes darkened and his smile faded slightly. "I think not. I think, Miss Benson, that you can very easily deduce my intent."

For the merest moment she was speechless. He was really coming on strong. Then she laughed again. "I don't have to deduce it," she told him gaily. "You've already stated it. Your intent—and mine—is to have fun."

He looked about to dispute this, but at that moment Marian Harrison appeared at the French doors. "Please come in now, everyone. Dinner is ready."

"It's been very nice talking to you," Hilary said, turning back to the big man beside her.

"Thank you," he said. "I'm glad you enjoyed it. Because you'll have to put up with me for a little longer."

"But dinner..."

"Dinner," he said, tucking her arm through his, "is exactly where we're going. And when we get there, I'll be sitting beside you." He lowered his voice. "Marian and I are old friends. I saw you coming in from the pasture this afternoon and when I heard you were going to be here this evening, I asked her to seat me next to you. I'm very tired of the company of the ladies I know." He helped her through the French doors and moved her toward the dining room. "I hope you don't mind my Machiavellian tactics," he said lightly, his eyes quizzical.

It did make her feel a little strange to know that their meeting had been arranged. But she found she was actually grateful. Some part of her had been dreading the dinner hour. Whatever wealthy people talked about during dinner, it was probably nothing *she* knew anything about. She would be lucky to remember to use her silver from the outside in. "No," she said. "I don't mind. You can tell me about race horses."

"I would much rather," he said quite seriously, "have you tell me about your training methods."

"Anything you want," Hilary said happily, raising her eyes to his face. "I aim to please."

She'd been so engrossed in Taylor that she had almost forgotten Justin. Now she saw him across the room, so darkly attractive in a dinner jacket that molded his strong shoulders. And on his left arm, clinging to him determinedly, was a petite brunette in a gown of scarlet satin that left very little to the imagination.

Justin raised his eyes just then, meeting hers, and she smiled and nodded pleasantly at him, as pleasantly as she could with the sudden pain churning inside her. There was Justin with a woman on his arm, a woman whose enormous dark eyes were rimmed with mascara and whose scarlet lips and nails matched her gown. Justin had better be careful, Hilary told herself cattily. Catching her glance, he frowned, his brows meeting. She looked carefully away.

"See someone you know?" Taylor asked.

"Just my boss. Over there with the little brunette in red."

"Ah, yes." For the first time Taylor's smile didn't reach his eyes. "Mitzi Drummond. The Scarlet Manager."

Hilary raised an eyebrow.

"It's a nickname," Taylor explained. "She favors that shade of scarlet. There's a bird, you know, the scarlet tanager. Well, one time someone called her the Scarlet Manager and the nickname stuck. Believe me, it fits."

"I wonder if she knows about it."

Taylor shrugged. "It doesn't make a lot of difference. If she does, she probably doesn't care. She's intent on managing herself into a marriage with some rich man."

"But she looks . . ." Hilary protested.

"Looks are not everything," Taylor said as they reached the dining room. "Though in your case..."

The warm glow caused by his compliment lasted while he seated her, then took his place at her right. To her left sat an older man whose name she could not remember. Justin was down the table on the other side. And beside him, still clinging, sat the Scarlet Manager, her great dark eyes never leaving Justin's face.

Hilary felt the surging of jealousy. Once *she* would have been at Justin's side, once his attention would have been all for *her*. If Justin married such a woman ... That thought hit her with such appalling force that she had to catch her breath. Well, bet or no bet, if that woman came to the Rocking J, Hilary Benson wasn't going to be around.

"Something wrong?" Taylor asked. "You look a little pale."

She managed a shaky smile. "Just excitement, I guess. Remember, I'm only a little old ranch girl. I'm not used to this high living."

Taylor's hearty laughter rang out again. From the corner of her eye she saw Justin turn and look at them. She smiled brightly at Taylor. "You!" Taylor said. "You're a fraud, Hilary Benson. You're the most beautiful, the most sophisticated woman in this room."

"Thank you, sir. You're very kind." Let Justin see she could enjoy herself, too.

"Kind nothing." His eyes were serious. "I mean that."

She was suddenly serious herself. "Yes, I guess you do. Thank you, Taylor."

The moment was broken by the waiters starting to serve and Hilary found herself with a hearty appetite. The food was excellent and Taylor's conversation was a pleasant addition to the meal.

By the time they had finished Marian's Kentucky cake Hilary was full. She leaned back in her chair and smiled at Taylor. "If I eat another bit, I'll burst."

"Don't do that," Taylor said. "There's dancing after dinner."

"Dancing?"

"Yes. Out under the Kentucky stars."

"You're kidding."

"Not me. I have it directly from Marian." His eyes traveled over her and he smiled. "It's not as nice as the Bahamas. No ocean, no beach. But with you here it won't matter."

She wasn't quite sure how to answer this. She liked Taylor; she liked him a lot. And he was fun. But she really knew very little about him. For all she knew, this was the way men of his class always behaved with women. Maybe his compliments and his admiring looks were just part of the usual course of things.

She was still debating this when Marian Harrison pushed back her chair. "Now, if you can still navigate after my Kentucky cake, there'll be dancing and drinks in the garden.''

"Shall we?" asked Taylor, his hand under her elbow.

"Yes, of course." She did not turn to look across the table at Justin and the woman who clung to him. She smiled up at Taylor instead. Could it be that Mitzi Drummond was the friend from whom Marian had heard of Justin's reputation? She tried to convince herself that it didn't really matter. The fact that she was still in love with Justin was unfortunate, but she would have to learn to handle it.

While they'd been at dinner, the patio and the adjoining garden had been transformed into a summer wonderland. Strings of Japanese lanterns hung from the trees and edged the pathways, and small candles in bright bowls flickered on the small white iron tables set around a space of patio floor that seemed designed for dancing.

The sweet strains of violins came floating through the air. "Perfect," said Taylor. "Would you like a drink?"

Hilary shook her head. He might as well know. "I don't drink, Taylor. Not at all."

He looked slightly bewildered. "But before..."

"Camouflage," she replied. "It's easier to carry one around than to keep explaining."

He nodded. "I see. Well, then. There'll be nothing to interfere with our dancing. Right?"

"Right."

His arm slid around her waist smoothly, drawing her nearer his big male body. Her cheek barely reached his shoulder and she felt dwarfed by his size. He lost no time in drawing her closely to him, and she did not pull back.

It was an evening made for dancing, made for being in a man's arms. The sweet scent of the garden flowers was all around them, and a little breeze ruffled Hilary's hair. It was like something out of the movies, she thought. The beautiful setting, the handsome man. A modern Cinderella story, she told herself, remembering the beautiful woman she had become. Except that it was the wrong man who held her in his arms. The wrong man whose chin rested against her hair, whose arms surrounded her so nicely.

She enjoyed Taylor, and she liked him a lot, but there was no feeling of madness, of wild anticipation. His body was very comfortable against hers, very male. But if it woke thoughts of something more, of passionate kisses and wild embraces, it was Justin's kisses and embraces that came to her mind and made her breath stick in her throat and her heart jump. She did not associate such things with Taylor. Not at all.

Still, there was a lot to be said for comfort. And the knowledge that Taylor really liked her made her feel very good, very feminine. She closed her eyes and let herself drift to the music, giving herself up to Taylor's deft guidance.

They danced for some time, only interrupted now and then by one of the other men cutting in on him. Taylor did nothing to stop this, except that within a minute or two he would be back, smiling pleasantly and cutting in himself.

"You don't mind, do you?" he asked, after this happened for the tenth time.

"No, I don't mind." She smiled slightly. She felt better than she had in months. Taylor's attentions were making a new woman of her.

"Here comes your boss," Taylor commented some time later. "Looks like he wants to talk to you."

She felt the whisper-light touch of his lips at her hairline. "See you later."

Then Justin reached her. Without a word he took her in his arms. And all the peace and happiness she'd been feeling deserted her. It was only with difficulty that she managed not to pull back, out of his arms, away from the body that had such a powerful hold on hers.

"So. It looks like you're enjoying yourself." The words, though softly spoken, sounded like an accusation.

She chose to ignore that. "Yes. I'm having a lovely time. Thank you for staying over. It's like a little vacation."

His grip on her hand tightened. "I thought we'd talk about the horses this evening."

"I knocked on your door when I came in from the pasture and before I came downstairs. You weren't there."

"I was busy."

"Of course," she said sweetly. "Does Miss Drummond raise horses?"

"Mitzi?" He looked surprised. "Of course not."

He drew her closer to him and she fought the waves of feeling that surged over her.

"That Taylor's been paying a lot of attention to you," he said, barely keeping his tone civil.

Something in her exulted. He *was* jealous! "Yes, he's been very kind. He raises horses, too, you know. The poor man lost his wife several years ago. He seems lonely."

Justin literally snorted. "The poor man, as you call him, could have any single woman on the Eastern Seaboard and half the married ones. There's no need to feel sorry for him."

"*Having* a woman," Hilary replied pointedly, "is not the same as loving her."

For a moment it seemed as though he would reply; she saw that muscle tense in his jaw. Then the closeness of his face became too much to bear and she turned away, looking out over his shoulder. There was a burr under Justin's saddle blanket, but she was not going to let it ruin her evening. This was the first fun she'd had in longer than she could remember.

She closed her eyes, wanting to give herself up to the music and the feel of Justin's body against hers. When she opened her eyes again she found that he had maneuvered her toward the dark end of the garden. "Justin, I . . ."

But he didn't respond to her pleas. His mouth came down and covered hers. She wanted to fight him, she really did. But her body would not listen to her. Her body wanted him and her lips softened under his, softened and parted.

His kiss left her breathless, leaning weakly against him. She tried to regain her sanity, tried to remember the awful thing he had done.

"Justin, darling. Where are you?" Mitzi Drummond's throaty voice, which reminded Hilary very much of a frog's croaking, sounded close by. Any moment now she would be coming around the screen of bushes that hid them.

A sudden madness overcame Hilary and instead of drawing away from him as she should have, she moved back into Justin's arms and raised her lips to his. His hesitation was only momentary. And then, though he must have guessed what would happen, he bent his head to hers again.

"Justy! Really!"

A smile hovered on Hilary's lips as Justin released her. "Hello, there, Miss Drummond," she said brightly. "Excuse me, Justin darling. I believe Taylor is looking for me."

And, conscious that both of them were staring after her, she returned to the lighted garden. There, she thought defiantly, let him explain that!

"Hilary." Miraculously, Taylor appeared beside her as she neared the house.

"Have you been watching me?" she asked in astonishment.

His eyes gleamed. "Of course. All evening. Ever since I met you. Listen—" his hand slid easily under her elbow "—how about a little walk? I've got some business to discuss with you."

"Business?" Hilary allowed herself to be maneuvered away from the lighted area and toward the farthest end of the garden. Thankfully, she did not see Justin or Mitzi nearby.

Taylor kept his hand on her elbow as though he were afraid he might lose her. As the music and the laughter faded behind them, she turned to him. "What kind of business, Taylor?"

"Horse business, what else?"

"What else," she echoed, wondering how any of this could be real.

Taylor led her toward a small white bench shining in the moonlight. "You train horses, right?"

"Right."

"Well, I have several horses I want you to work with."

"But I don't train race horses."

"I don't exactly want you to train them," he continued, settling beside her on the bench. "I want you to *untrain* them. They've got some bad habits that need changed. From what you told me at dinner you're just the person to do it.''

"But it would take too long. I can't leave Montana. I have a contract with Justin."

"Did I say anything about leaving Montana?" He smiled at her.

"No, but your horses... They're in Kentucky, aren't they?"

He nodded. "Yes, they are. But if you'll agree to do the job, I'll have them flown out."

"Flown?" This was all moving so fast.

"I have a special plane for the job," he said softly. "They're used to it."

"Flown," she repeated numbly.

"You can keep them as long as necessary. And I'll pay whatever fee you charge. Plus room and board, of course."

"Of course." She felt stupid, echoing his words like this, but she couldn't seem to think straight. "I can't promise to cure them," she said hurriedly. "There are a few horses that nothing can be done with."

"I have confidence in your ability," he said, taking her hand in his and opening it so that it lay palm up and his big fingers could trace lacy patterns there. "Just say you'll do it," he said. "We can settle the details later."

"Yes, yes. I'll do it." She would work them in somewhere. The extra money would mean a lot, but even more helpful would be the prestige. If Taylor sent his horses to her, others in his group might follow. And the Circle K would have a new source of income.

"And now," said Taylor softly, his arm stealing around her waist, "that's settled. There are other things on my mind."

"What . . ." she began, but got no further before his lips met hers. She was not exactly surprised. Taylor had made no secret of the fact that he was attracted to her.

But it was disconcerting to be discussing the training of his horses one minute, and to have the man kissing her the next. And doing a very good job of it, too, she thought as she found herself responding. It was not like being kissed by Justin. There were no shooting fireworks, no earthshaking tremors. But it was a very satisfying kiss, nevertheless.

When Taylor broke off the kiss, his arm stayed around her waist. "I hope you aren't going to be angry with me," he said. "I've been wanting to do that since the first moment I laid eyes on you. Just think how long I've been restraining myself."

She had to laugh then. He looked so appealing. He was good for her, she thought as his mouth descended once more. Maybe this was what she needed. Maybe it was Taylor who could make her forget Justin, make her life happy again. She wrapped her arms around his neck and returned his kiss. It was certainly worth a try.

Seven

The musicians played well into the wee hours of the morning. By that time, most of the other guests had wandered off, some to drive home, some to sleep in the rooms Marian Harrison provided for them.

Hilary noticed when Justin and Mitzi Drummond slipped off. It was hard not to, since Miss Drummond seemed determined to let the whole world know, calling good night in her throaty voice clear across the room.

Hilary fought the wave of panic that hit her as she saw them leave the garden together, laughing. Unconsciously, she moved closer to Taylor, to the comfort of his body.

"Tired?" he asked, his eyes smiling at her warmly. "We could stop dancing."

"No," she replied, managing a smile. "I love dancing with you." And, indeed, that was true. It was not like dancing with Justin. With Taylor everything was comfortable and safe. With Justin it was wild and glorious. But Justin wasn't there.

And so they danced on and on until finally everyone else had gone and the musicians, looking apologetic, packed up their instruments. Still smiling, Taylor took her back to her room and outside her door kissed her soundly.

Finally Taylor drew back. "I'm very attracted to you," he said softly. "I don't suppose I have to tell you that."

She smiled. "No, I guess not."

"But I'm also very old-fashioned. So, much as I want to, I won't ask to spend the night with you."

"Thank you." The words came out smoothly over the sudden lump in her throat, and she was grateful she could have such self-control. "That's good. Because I'm old-fashioned, too, and I couldn't."

His grin was the most endearing thing. "I didn't think you would," he said. "Listen, I have to go home tonight. I wish I didn't, but I do. I'll get your address and phone number from Marian. I'll be in touch. You can count on it."

He looked about to take her in his arms once more, then with a sigh he drew back. "I'd better not kiss you again," he said ruefully. "Or I may forget how old-fashioned I am."

"Good night, Taylor. Thank you for a lovely evening."

"Thank *you*," he said before he turned and hurried away.

Later, with the borrowed dress hanging once more in the closet and wearing the borrowed nightgown she had found waiting for her on the turned-down bed, Hilary lay staring into the darkness. What an incredible day it had been. To think that this morning she'd been a horse trainer in Montana and tonight she was the most beautiful woman in Taylor Morris's world. The thought was exhilarating.

She stretched luxuriously, feeling the smooth silk of the gown against her skin. No wonder women liked to wear silk, she thought. It made her feel deliciously female, and slightly wicked.

Carefully, she examined her feelings about Taylor. He was a very nice man. Very attractive, too. And he certainly knew how to treat a woman. She smiled. He had made her feel very good and very feminine.

There was no doubt in her mind that he would be a gentle, accomplished lover. For a moment she found herself regretting his old-fashioned ways. But then she sighed. Taylor had been right to wait. It was far too soon for them to do something like that. Besides, there was no way she could make love to

Taylor knowing that Justin might be in the next room.

Now if that had been Justin kissing her good-night, like he used to... Well, it wouldn't have been good-night. Justin would have come into the room with her and she wouldn't have been lying alone in this gigantic bed.

Suddenly all her good feelings fled. A lump of tears swelled in her throat. If Taylor had still been there, she would have grabbed at him, begged him to spend the night with her regardless of what he felt. For now it was impossible not to think of Justin, not to remember that very real kiss in the garden. It was his body she could feel against her own, his breath on her forehead, his arms holding her close.

"I've got to get over him," she told herself fiercely. "I've got to. Oh, Taylor, please call me soon. Very soon."

She cried for a while, silent tears that coursed down her cheeks and dampened the expensive sheets. But she could not cry herself to sleep. Finally, not knowing what else to do, she stumbled into the bathroom and rummaged in the medicine cabinet for the over-the-counter sleeping pills she had seen there earlier. She swallowed two and crawled back into bed. And then, exhausted by the day that had begun before dawn, and that had held so much excitement, she finally drifted off.

Her sleep was not peaceful, of course. How could it be when it was full of dreams of Justin? "I love you," he said in that deep Northern voice that thrilled her. "I love you very much. And I'm going to prove it. Right now."

The bed appeared in her dream, the big canopied bed in her Kentucky bedroom. And Justin was in it beside her, his body against her own. She felt his wild kisses on her face, her neck, against her mouth. She moaned, wanting him, wanting him with an ache that couldn't be satisfied.

In her dream she heard the knocking on her door, Justin's insistent voice crying, "Hilary, Hilary. Let me in!"

She scrambled to her feet, only half awake, and stumbled to the door.

Justin stood there. His evening tie was askew, his jacket unbuttoned. His rumpled hair hung down on his forehead, but not far enough to hide the meeting of his dark brows. "Let me in," he demanded. "Let me in."

"What do you want?" she stammered, still befuddled by sleep.

"You," he said, his voice husky with desire. "I want you." His words pulled at her, desire filled her body. His hands came down hard on her bare shoulders, pushing aside the gown's thin straps, baring her skin. He bent his head, his lips moving roughly over her smoothness. The moan came from her throat without her volition. His fingers were busy, stripping the delicate lace of the gown down to reveal her quivering breasts, their rosy peaks yearning for the touch of his hand.

He stared at them for one long moment. "God," he said huskily. "It's been such a long time."

"Yes, oh yes," she murmured as he bent his head to kiss the softness he'd revealed. She wanted him so much. Nothing else seemed to matter. His hands pulled at the gown impatiently, pushing it farther down until it fell to the floor, a silken pool around her bare feet.

He crushed her against him for a moment, his mouth covering hers in a kiss that sent her whole body soaring into ecstasy. Then he swung her up into his arms and carried her to the bed.

He kissed her again, his lips like fire on her own, his tongue taking possession of her mouth, before he put her down among the tumbled pillows.

Her breasts heaving, she watched through half-closed eyes as he took off his clothes. He threw his shirt to one side, heedless of where it fell, and she let her eyes rest on the expanse of his bare chest, lightly covered with dark hair that arrowed downward and disappeared into the trousers he was unbelting. They dropped to his feet and his shorts followed. She drew in her breath at the strong male sight of him.

Then his body hit the bed with such force that the springs protested, and he rolled toward her, gathering her tightly in his arms.

Another moan escaped as his body met hers, as his hands curled in the mass of her hair and his mouth possessed hers with a savagery that found an answering response deep within her.

His mouth seemed to be everywhere at once, on her face, on her throat, on the smooth curve of her shoulder, the soft slope of breast. Across the flat plain of her stomach it moved, leaving a path of flaming desire behind it, down to her most secret places, where it lingered, driving her closer and closer to the ultimate fulfillment.

"Justin," she moaned, "oh, Justin."

He covered her yearning body with his own and she arched up against him, needing him, needing desperately to be one with him.

It was good, so good, she thought. Better even than she remembered it.

His hands under her shoulders gathered her to him with a force that left her already breathless lungs struggling for air. Then he was in her, and all thought left her mind. There was nothing but the wild beauty of their mating. It was like riding the swiftest stallion, only a hundred, a thousand, times better. She soared, her body in a flight of ecstasy, not bound by space or time.

Her hands gripped his shoulders, clutching at him as though she could hold this moment forever. She heard the harsh explosion of breath that had always signaled his release and her own body exploded up there in the sky, slowly falling back to earth in millions of shining fragments.

Slowly her breathing returned to normal. And, as it did, her mind returned to sanity. Her body had betrayed her, had made her give in to her passion. She was suddenly ill, filled with self-loathing. To have made love with the man who had killed her father!

She pushed at his arm that held her close against him. "Justin, Justin."

"Huh?" He was hanging on the edge of sleep, so comfortable, so satisfied. In spite of that Morris character he had managed it. He, Justin Porter, was the one in bed with her.

"Justin," Hilary repeated, her voice growing more impatient.

The sudden change in the feel of her body alerted him as much as the sharpness of her tone. "What is it, honey?" He moved to kiss her, but she turned her face away.

"Get up. Go back to your own room." Her voice was strangely flat.

"Don't worry about the Harrisons," he said. "Didn't Marian put us next to each other?"

She twisted, trying to escape from his arms, and he felt his desire igniting again.

"I don't care about Marian," she cried. "I want you out of here!"

The vehemence of her tone startled him. A minute ago she'd been the old Hilary, as wildly and passionately involved in their lovemaking as he was. "I don't understand, honey. I thought . . ."

His use of the endearment infuriated her. "You thought you could do just as you pleased. Well, think again. Get out of here."

"I can't believe this. What's wrong with you?" She'd come to him willingly enough, passionately enough. She had done everything and clearly enjoyed it. Only now she was boiling mad.

She glared at him. "What's wrong? You know damn well what's wrong! You know what you did to my father."

Suddenly galvanized, he leaped to his feet and started gathering up his clothes. "The same old argument. I didn't do anything. The old man killed himself."

"Just get away from me! Get out." She clutched the sheet to her. "You...you..." Words failed her and she could only glare at him.

As he yanked on his shorts, she averted her eyes from his nakedness. She must be losing her mind, she thought grimly, to have done this terrible thing.

"You opened the door," he said. "You wanted me." He took a step toward her, back toward the bed.

"I . . . I . . . I had too much to drink," she stammered. "It was a very romantic evening. I got carried away. It was sex. Nothing more."

She saw his brows draw together. "It's still there, Hilary. The fire between us. You know that. Why can't we be like we used to be?"

"We can't. You know we can't!" Panic rose to almost choke her. If he touched her again . . . God, how she wanted him, wanted him still. "Get out. And don't think this will happen again because it won't. What we had is over. Dead." She choked on the harsh word, thinking of Papa and their dreams. "Gone."

He jerked on his trousers, his face white under his tan.

Her fingers ached where they clutched the sheet. "I'm going to forget this ever happened. You forget it, too. Now get out!"

Her tears were very near the surface now, but she managed to hold them back, to sit in stony-faced silence while he gathered the rest of his clothes. "Very well," he said finally, his face set and that little muscle twitching in his jaw. "If you want to go on pretending. I can't stop you. Just remember, I know better."

His eyes burned into hers. Papa, she reminded herself. Think what he did to Papa.

"We'll talk about the horses in the morning," he said calmly. Then he went out, closing the door quietly behind him.

Hilary collapsed among the tangled bedclothes. "What have I done?" she sobbed. "What *have* I done?"

In the room next door an exasperated Justin stripped off his trousers and threw himself onto the bed. He was angry, but one fact overrode all others, and finally it let him fall asleep with a smile on his face. Whatever she said, whatever excuse she had made afterward, Hilary had welcomed him with open arms. The fire was still there, and given that he would win her.

It was late the next morning when Hilary finally got up and dressed. It had been dawn before she was able to calm herself enough to rest. For hours and hours she lay there, thinking, trying unsuccessfully to sort out her confused emotions.

She gave the green gown a wistful glance before she shut the closet door. Everything else that had been loaned her, including the silk nightgown that had been lying on the floor when she woke, a mute reminder of the night's madness, she had put neatly on the velvet covered chaise lounge. She picked up her bag, then, straightening her shoulders and wishing that her eyes didn't look so bad, so red and puffy, she set out for the breakfast room.

The room was empty, but the sound of voices from the veranda indicated that some guests were breakfasting outdoors. She filled her plate and moved toward the sound. Too bad Taylor wasn't still here. She was badly in need of some of his kindness.

"Good morning, Hilary." Marian Harrison's eyes rested shrewdly on her face for a moment, then she averted them politely. "I hope you slept well."

"A little late, I'm afraid." She managed a small laugh, relieved to see that Justin was not among those sitting at the veranda table.

"They went out to look at the horses again," Marian said. "I hear you like Pocahontas."

"Your medicine-hat paint?" Hilary asked. "Yes, she's a beauty. It'll be interesting to see what sort of foals she throws."

If only she could get home some other way, she thought. How could she meet Justin face-to-face in front of all these people? But even worse, how could she be alone with him after what had happened?

Fortunately, the few remaining guests were intent on other things and she was able to eat without having to make polite conversation. She was just sipping her second cup of coffee when Justin and Peter Harrison returned. "Good morning," said Peter, a little too heartily.

"Good morning." She wanted to keep her gaze away from Justin's face, but her eyes were drawn there anyway. To her surprise, he did not look any different than he had the day before. It was almost as though last night hadn't happened.

"Good morning, Hilary," he said. "Peter and I have been out to look at the horses. I've got all the details now." He smiled at their host. "We'll discuss them on the way home and I'll get back to you."

"Fine."

As she put down her cup and got to her feet, Peter Harrison once more extended his hand. "It's been good meeting you, Hilary. I hope you'll come back and visit us again some time. Not necessarily to buy horses."

"Thank you." She forced herself to say the proper polite words. "Thank you, Marian, for the lovely room and the use of the clothes."

Marian shrugged. "It was no trouble at all, Hilary. I was glad to do it."

Half an hour later, they were in the air, heading toward Montana. Hilary tried to keep her eyes closed. If only she could sleep until they got home, until she didn't have to be alone with him. But she couldn't relax. When her eyes were closed, she felt that he was looking at her, that he was remembering last night. But when she opened them, he was looking out at the sky or down at his instruments.

She swallowed a sigh. They couldn't go on like this, sitting in silence all the way back to Montana.

Keeping his eyes carefully away from her, Justin tried to think what to do next. This was hardly an appropriate time to start a discussion of last night, while he was piloting a plane. Besides, what good would it do? Hilary was convinced that he had killed her old man. He almost snorted, thinking of it. That old cowboy could have drunk anyone under the table. And as for gambling... It was a wonder he hadn't staked his own daughter on a bet.

Forget it, he told himself wryly. But he couldn't forget their lovemaking: her touch, her smell, her feel. The wonder of it. He let his mind roam. He'd come on a little strong when she opened the door, but he couldn't help that. Taylor Morris hadn't left her side all evening, and with Mitzi hanging on him like a leech, he'd been unable to do much about it. It was a wonder he'd managed that one dance, that stolen kiss.

If he had found Morris in her room... Well, thankfully he hadn't. He'd been spared committing assault and battery on one of the East Coast's wealthiest men.

He'd certainly been wild with jealousy when he got to her door. Jealousy was a new emotion to him; one he didn't care for at all. And she had been so beautiful.

He swallowed a smile. The green dress had been lovely on her. But in that silk nightgown... He felt the stirring of desire again. God, how he loved this woman. It was weird, because they were so different. Before, he'd thought he knew her, could understand her. Events had proved to him that that simply wasn't so. But there was one thing he was damn sure of.

He loved Hilary Benson. With all her wild crazy ways, he loved her. The past year without her had been pure hell. Last night might not prove that she loved him, like she'd said that time he'd found her dreaming in the stable. But it sure meant she wanted him. And that gave him something to build on.

He took a deep breath and steadied his voice. "So," he said. "Tell me what you think about the stallion. Can you really cure him and will it be worth our while?"

It took Hilary a moment to pull her thoughts together, to pull them away from the night before. "I don't see any problem," she said, trying to make her voice as businesslike as his. "He's got great lines. His stud record is good. He probably cribs from boredom. That's a minor problem."

"And his habit of 'nipping back pockets'?" The phrase brought to mind a picture of *her* lovely behind, and he dismissed it quickly. It was just business this morning. She was making that pretty clear.

"I think I know what caused that," she said, grateful to be able to talk like this, as though last night were a bad dream. "That's why I wanted to be alone with him."

"You did go into that pasture!" He shot her an angry look.

"Of course I did. How else was I supposed to make friends with the horse?"

"And I suppose you walked right up to him and blew into his nostrils?"

"Not quite," she replied. "I just went inside the fence. He came to me."

Justin turned to stare at her. At least she was talking to him, even if it was only about horses. "I thought Peter said he was shy."

"He did. That's why I only went a little way inside the fence. Then I turned my back to him and started singing."

"You turned your back on a strange stallion," he repeated, shaking his head.

"Yes. It worked, too. He got curious and came around to see what I was doing. *Then* I blew into his nostrils." She smiled. "He's really a very nice horse."

"And did he nip your back pocket?" He couldn't help asking the question.

"No," she said quietly. "He pulled out the hankie I had put there and presented it to me. It's a game he learned to play, probably when he was little."

"Can you teach him not to play it now?"

"Yes," she said. "But it might be better not to. It might be better if everyone who dealt with him kept a hankie in his back pocket."

"You've got to be kidding."

She smiled at his indignation. "Not really. He enjoys it and he'll feel kindly toward anyone who plays the game with him."

Justin shook his head, but he was smiling. "The foals aren't allowed to wear halters and the trainers have to carry handkerchiefs. We're going to be the laughingstock of Montana."

"Nobody laughed at Papa," she said quietly. "Not after they saw what he'd accomplished. He could do anything with a horse." Her voice grew steely. "If you don't like my methods, you can always let me go."

"I'm not going to do that," he said immediately, his jaw tightening. "When I make a bet, I stick to it. Now, what about the mares?"

"The seal brown, for sure," she replied. "She's the best of the lot. The sorrel wasn't bad. Or the slate. Actually, they were all pretty good looking, but I think those three are the best. Which one do you plan to buy?"

"The seal brown certainly," he said. "Do you think we can accommodate the other two?"

"There's plenty of stable room. But you have to consider winter feed and training time for their foals."

The rest of the flight home was spent discussing the acquisition of the new stock. As Hilary climbed out of the plane some hours later, she heaved a sigh of relief. She badly needed some time alone with her horses. She might tell herself again and again that last night had been a mistake, that she wasn't going to think about it anymore. But confined in that small plane with him, being so close to him, she had been unable to follow her own advice.

Accepting her shoulder bag, she said, "If someone will just drive me home, I'll see you tomorrow."

"Right. Sandy will drive you. Thank you for going with me," he said as she moved toward the truck. "I really appreciate your help."

"You're welcome," she replied. "I think we should do very well with this new stock."

He nodded. She had said *we*. He liked the sound of that. He especially liked the fact that she wasn't even aware she'd said it. Yes, he thought as he watched her climb into the truck with Sandy, the trip had been worthwhile. If it hadn't worked out exactly as he had planned, well, it had worked to a degree. He'd just have to be patient a little longer. At least now they were home he wouldn't have to contend with that Morris.

God, the man made him see red. The thought of that color brought to mind Mitzi Drummond in that red silk gown. Mitzi had a great body. There was no denying that. And perhaps she'd been partially justified in supposing that he would want to avail himself of its charms once again. She'd certainly given it the old college try, even laughing off the kiss Hilary had deliberately prolonged. But the woman was so artificial, he thought. In contrast to Hilary, Mitzi looked fake and insincere. He shook his head as he set off toward the ranch house.

Of course, he hadn't counted on Taylor Morris making such a play for Hilary. Or, he thought with a frown, on her being so taken with him. Well, she hadn't slept with the man. That much he knew.

Some minutes later a tired Hilary opened the door to the ranch house and gasped. The living room looked like a garden. Six dozen red roses filled the room with their fragrance. She turned to the man behind her. "Jeb, what on earth is this?"

"I had to stick 'em in cans," he said, grinning widely. "They all came this morning. And a telegram, too. It's over there on the table."

Hilary opened it with trembling fingers. "Hope you like roses," she read. "They remind me of you. Will call tonight. Love, Taylor."

Eight

Two weeks later Hilary stood outside the corral fence, watching Betsy's Barracuda. It had not taken the stallion long to become accustomed to his Montana home. Thinking of the sign they had put over his stall, she smiled. "Attention," it read. "When handling this horse, be sure to leave a handkerchief hanging out of your back pocket."

BB, as she had affectionately nicknamed him, liked anyone who would play his game and eventually every man on the ranch had given in to curiosity and come around to see the stallion do his trick.

Hilary smiled to herself as he pranced happily over to the fence and whuffled a friendly hello.

With so many new friends all willing to play, the stallion had forgotten his previous shyness.

She stroked the smooth softness of his neck. "You're a lovely horse," she crooned as he leaned over the fence to put his head against her cheek. "A lovely, lovely horse. If only people were as smart as you."

"Me, in particular," she added with a sigh. The past two weeks had been the strangest of her life. Since their return from Kentucky they'd been very busy; on top of training the foals, they had to get ready for the new arrivals, and make them comfortable when they got there. That was the kind of work Hilary was used to. What was so strange was working side by side with Justin, sharing so many moments together, and neither of them ever referring to what had happened between them that night. She knew that she had said she meant to pretend it had never happened, but, somehow, she hadn't expected him to do the same.

And then, every night, every single night since she'd arrived home to find the living room full of roses, Taylor had called. Not just to say hello. They had talked each night for nearly an hour, talked and laughed, and gotten to know each other. And now he was planning to fly out, to make arrangements for the horses he wanted her to work with. At least, that was ostensibly the reason for his trip. She was quite sure there was more to it than that.

She sighed as the stallion pushed his soft nose into her palm. If only people were as simple to deal with as horses, life would certainly be a lot easier. Taylor would be arriving in three days. He wanted to fly into Justin's airstrip, which was closer to the Circle K than any other. But how was Justin going to react to that? He had not been exactly blind to Taylor's attentions to her. It seemed clear, too, that he didn't like Taylor.

Hilary frowned. If only she wasn't feeling so confused about everything. *She* liked Taylor; he was a very likable man. But her memories of the time they'd spent together were obscured by the passion she had shared with Justin.

It was very nice to be courted like this. To come home to a house full of fragrant flowers. To receive long-distance phone calls from a man every night. She would be foolish not to enjoy it.

But Justin could not be forgotten. He was always there, working beside her every day. And there was no way she could deny it to herself; she wanted him. She wanted him as badly as she ever had.

Justin and Taylor: two men who wanted her. How different they were. It was not just a matter of looks—Justin's dark looks or Taylor's blond ones. Or of the way they behaved. Justin's everyday businesslike tone and the rough way he had burst into her room contrasted to Taylor's lovely romantic wooing and thoughtful abstinence. There was more to it than that.

She sighed again and the stallion eyed her curiously. She was just so bewildered. She ought to be able to make up her mind. She wanted to get over Justin, and Taylor was obviously the right choice. He loved and respected her. He was very good looking and attentive. To say nothing of his money. That really wasn't the issue, of course. Justin was just as wealthy, and, anyway, she wasn't into money. She wasn't like Mitzi Drummond. And she would never accept anyone's help with the Circle K. It was her ranch, and it would stay that way.

Yes, she thought, it ought to be clear to anyone that she was a very lucky woman. P. Taylor Morris was a wonderful man. He even loved horses.

But at night, after their talks, when she lay in her lonely bed trying to get to sleep, it was not Taylor whom she thought about. It was Justin's dark face that was always before her eyes, his lean body that she yearned for. At those times, when she remembered Kentucky, it was not dancing under the stars in Taylor's arms that filled her mind, but those mad moments of passion in the canopied bed, moments shared with the man responsible for her father's death. She loved Justin. There was no question of that. And he still loved her. But how could anything ever come of their love? How could she forget what he had done to her father?

"How could I have slept with him?" she asked the stallion. "How *could* I have?"

The stallion's amber eyes regarded her silently, and Hilary sighed again. "Well, at least you're doing well. And your new ladies, too."

The mares had been given a few days to recover from the trip, but it didn't seem to have bothered them much. Vic had checked them over and pronounced them all healthy and ready to become mothers. BB had already covered the seal brown and the slate was scheduled for next week. The trip had worked out well in that regard, at least.

If only the year was over, she thought. If only she could get away from Justin. Go off some place with Taylor. He would like that, she knew. They could relax and have fun. Forget all the pain and turmoil. But how could she do that? This was only her second month as Justin's trainer.

"You really were right about him," Justin said, coming up silently from behind her and leaning against the fence.

She trembled as his arm brushed hers and she swallowed hastily, trying to blank out memories of that passionate night. "Yes, he's a beautiful animal. Very well-mannered."

Justin's chuckle surprised her. "I hear the ranchers hereabouts have given him a new name."

"Oh?" Her duties at both places kept her so busy that she seldom got into town and Taylor's calls had cut short whatever evening conversations she might have had with Jeb.

"Yes, they're calling him the Handkerchief Horse. I imagine we could sell tickets."

"Another source of income for the Rocking J," Hilary said with a lightness she didn't feel. It had been hard talking to Justin before, with the memories of their past love in her mind. But now, with their recent passionate mating searing through her, she found it doubly difficult.

"I don't think we'll be forced to that," he said, matching her tone. "The Rocking J is in pretty good shape."

"I'm glad to hear that." She might as well get it over with, she told herself. There was no use putting it off. "I, ah, I have a favor to ask of you."

He turned toward her so softly that she was startled and the stallion shied away, his dark eyes flicking.

"Of course," Justin said, his eyes searching her face. "What is it?"

"Ah..." She was finding it really hard going, especially since she felt she had to look at him while she talked. "I have a client. Someone who's sending me some horses to train." She saw the disappointment on his face. What kind of favor had he thought she wanted? "It won't interfere with my work here. This client knows about that." Why couldn't she say his name? she asked herself. Just blurt it out?

"They want to fly in to check things out and they'd like to use your landing strip. It's the closest."

His brows had been drawing together while she talked and now they met in the middle of his forehead, giving him that dark, foreboding look she had learned to dread. "What is this client's name?"

"He's a friend of Peter Harrison. P. Taylor Morris."

"I see." He was proud of himself, he thought. And he had a right to be. It took real self-control not to give vent to the rage he was feeling at the thought of that man coming here. "When does Morris plan to arrive?"

"I think Friday afternoon. If that's all right with you, of course."

"Of course." He'd better be careful, he thought. He couldn't keep up this kind of pretense for too long. He'd like to strangle the man. As for Hilary... What he'd like to do to her sent his blood racing. "Yes," he continued, concentrating on keeping a nice quiet, calm tone. "That should be fine. Give Taylor my regards."

He forced himself to look slowly at his watch, to smile and say, "I'll talk to you later. I'm expecting a call." He even managed to walk away normally, not to reach out and crush her to him, not to demand that she admit to their love.

So Taylor Morris was coming to Montana. Well, that was just too bad. Hilary belonged to Justin

Porter. He had not waited patiently all these long months to have her stolen from under his very nose.

The worst of it, he thought unhappily as he stormed into the ranch house and threw himself into a chair, was that actually, in his saner moments, he liked Taylor Morris. The man was a decent human being and in other circumstances they might even have become friends. But he can't have Hilary, he told himself angrily. She loves me. She's mine.

On Friday afternoon, waiting by Justin's landing strip with Brandy and another saddled horse for Taylor, Hilary was decidedly uncomfortable. The past three days had been miserable ones. Justin had seemed like another person, so determinedly bright and cheerful, but with such an ominous look around his eyes that she hardly knew how to deal with him. His phony cheerfulness didn't fool her, especially since in moments of stress it tended to slip, revealing a boiling rage all out of proportion to whatever little setback had seemingly caused it.

She would have given a great deal during those days to know whether Justin intended to be present when the plane landed. But she hadn't dared to ask him. The subject of Taylor had become as forbidden as their passionate night at the Harrison's.

Hilary pushed her Stetson to the back of her head and sighed. She hoped Taylor would not be put off by the Circle K. She had tried to warn him, tried to let him know that hers was a very small operation.

She had even tried to warn him, in a roundabout way, about Justin.

She sighed as she looked down at her faded jeans and scuffed boots. She hoped Taylor wouldn't be disappointed when he saw her. She didn't look much like the beautiful, green-gowned woman he had danced with in Kentucky, and she had no fancy clothes to put on for him.

He would have to get used to her the way she was, she thought. This, after all, was the real Hilary Benson, not the elegantly gowned woman he had found so attractive.

Though she felt she knew him very well—hadn't they been on the phone every night for two weeks—she had still only actually spent that one evening with him and that had been a magic, romantic evening, very removed from the usual everydayness of her life.

She swallowed another sigh and absently stroked Brandy's flank. She was still just as confused about things as ever. Right now she could only hope that Taylor would be on time and that Justin would be busy elsewhere. Then maybe they wouldn't have to meet.

The horses shifted their weight and Brandy turned to look back over his shoulder. She knew, without looking herself, that Justin was approaching. Her body's response to his nearness was always predictable.

"What time is your client arriving?" Justin asked, swinging down from the roan that he usually rode and tethering it beside Brandy.

"Any time now," she replied, trying to ignore the emphasis he had put on the word client. "He said around five."

"Well, he has nice weather for flying." Justin turned his eyes to the blue Montana sky, which at that moment was completely free of clouds.

"Yes," Hilary agreed, following his gaze. "It's a lovely day." How sad, she thought, that now they were reduced to discussing such banalities as the weather, and after what the two of them had shared.

Please, she prayed silently. Make Taylor hurry up and get here. I can't take much more of this.

"Will you be late to work on Monday?" Justin asked.

She had not meant to look at him directly, but his question startled her so that she turned. "Of course not. Why should I be?"

"I thought you might be spending extra time with your client." His face remained set in hard lines, but there was a definite sneer in his voice.

"I told you, Taylor's only coming for the weekend." She tried to be patient, but this jealousy of his was ridiculous. "I won't be taking any time off. I'll even be working with Golden Lady as usual." His eyes were so hard, so angry. She suppressed a shiver. "I didn't contract for weekends, you know."

This attitude of his was beginning to get to her. "You don't own my soul."

"Don't worry," he snapped. "I'm very much aware of that." Then suddenly he seemed to realize his sharpness and he smiled sheepishly. "I'm sorry about that, Hilary. I'm afraid I'm not myself this week. I've got some tough decisions to make. A lot on my mind."

He really looked awful, she thought, now that she was actually looking at him and not avoiding his eyes as she had all week. There were new worry lines around his eyes and his mouth looked... She searched her mind for the right word. He looked almost wounded. "Is it the ranch?" she asked softly, forgetting the past in a rush of sympathy for this man who had meant so much to her. "Can I help?"

He smiled ruefully. "I'm afraid not. But thanks." This was not the time, he cautioned himself. Not the time to make her talk about that night in Kentucky and the passion they had shared.

No wonder he looked worried, he thought wryly. He'd been awake half the night, tortured by memories of their love, of their wonderful times together. Tortured, too, by the thought that P. Taylor Morris was going to spend two nights at the Circle K, two nights alone in the house with Hilary. And there was not a damned thing he could do about it. Not one damn thing.

The whine of the approaching engine made them both look up, though he noticed that Hilary's eyes went first to the horses. Accustomed to the sound, they remained placidly waiting. Almost against his will, he watched Hilary's face. There was excitement there, he could see that. But was there love?

He clamped down on his feelings and averted his gaze. It wasn't good to look too long at her face. Or any other part of her, he thought angrily.

The little jet glided to a smooth stop. Grudgingly, Justin admired the pilot's skill. Then the door opened and Taylor climbed out. "Hilary!"

Justin was conscious of disappointment. Somewhere in the back of his mind he had hoped that Taylor would appear in his business suit, or wearing something that would make him look ridiculous or inappropriate. But no such luck. The man was wearing standard Western gear, and he looked really good in it.

While Justin watched helplessly, this interloper came toward her, his duffel bag over his shoulder, his face alight with the pleasure of seeing her.

"Hilary! It's so good to see you again." And he enveloped her in a giant bear hug.

Justin's jaw clamped down so hard he could feel the pain in the top of his head.

When Taylor released her, he turned to Justin. "It's really good of you to let me land here. Saves me a lot of time and trouble."

"It's nothing," said Justin, somehow managing a polite tone. "Glad to do you the favor."

He doesn't look glad, thought Hilary, he looks murderous. As though he can barely remain polite.

"I can't thank you enough for bringing Hilary to Kentucky," Taylor said, putting an arm around her and pulling her close. "It was the most marvelous thing to meet her. Gave me a whole new lease on life."

Hilary, standing within the circle of Taylor's arm, saw Justin fighting to retain his civility. But he had no right to be jealous. She had to get on with her life. And she couldn't spend it with the man who had caused her father's death. She swallowed a sigh. If only it didn't have to be this way.

"Hilary's very good with horses," Justin said, the effort he was making clearly visible to her anxious eyes. He glanced hurriedly at his watch. "Sorry to have to run, but I have an appointment in town. Enjoy your stay in Montana."

"Thank you . . ." Taylor began, but Justin had already swung up on his roan and was galloping off.

Taylor frowned. "I hope I haven't offended the man. He seems angry about something."

Hilary tugged at his hand. "He'll be all right. He's probably worried about some business deal."

Taylor's frown vanished as he turned to her. "I can't tell you how happy I am to see you." His eyes traveled over her. "You look absolutely marvelous. More beautiful than ever."

She laughed, thinking of her silly fears. "Oh, Taylor, you're a terrible flatterer. But I have to admit that I like it."

"I am not flattering you," he said stoutly as he followed her to the horses and tied his duffel bag behind the saddle. "You're truly a beautiful woman. Without—and within."

The sincerity in his voice was real and somehow she couldn't laugh away this compliment. "Thank you, Taylor. You're very sweet."

"I mean to be," he said softly. "But nevertheless what I said was true."

He moved around to the front of the horse, a chestnut mare named Ginger, and blew softly into her nostrils.

Hilary stared at him in surprise. "How... Who taught you to do that?"

"You forget." His grin was boyish. "I'm a man of means. In these past two weeks I've hardly been able to think of anything but you. I wanted to know everything I could about you."

"But..."

"One of my trainers once worked with your father. He told me about the greeting. He told me about other things, too."

"I..." She saw by the look on his face that he knew about Papa, about Papa's death. "Please, Taylor, not here. I don't want to talk about it. Not now."

"Of course," he said quietly, reaching out to take her hand in his. "I just want you to know that I'm your friend. You can tell me anything, Hilary. Anything at all."

"I . . ." The tears threatened to choke her. "Th-thank you."

She turned from him, quickly mounting Brandy, welcoming the familiar solid feel of the gelding between her legs. "Maybe we'll talk later. But for now, let's go home."

"That has a nice ring to it," Taylor said, as he swung gracefully into the saddle. "I'm glad you suggested we ride to your place. I'm busy so much of the time that I hardly get the chance to ride. And I do enjoy it."

"I thought riding home would give you a chance to see the prairie," she said, smiling. "Also, from the more practical point of view, we only have one vehicle that's running now and it belongs to Jeb, my foreman."

"I see." His eyes searched her face, but he didn't go back to the subject of her father.

"Tell me about the horses you want me to work with," she went on. "What sort of vices do they have?"

He looked at her closely. "All right, Hilary. I'll humor you now. But I give you fair warning. Once our horse business is taken care of, I have other, more important, things to discuss."

She didn't ask him what those things were. She couldn't; her heart had risen up in her throat and was threatening to choke her.

Nine

The fire in the ranch house fireplace was unnecessary. It was, after all, summer. But the evenings could be cool and Hilary liked a fire. It was a long while since she had had the time to light one—or to sit and enjoy it. But she had decided that during Taylor's short visit, she would keep her ranch work to the minimum.

Now, sitting beside him on the sofa, she stared into the flames. Soon he was going to bring up those important things he'd mentioned earlier. They'd already discussed his problem horses; there was nothing wrong with them that she couldn't cure. Then she had showed him around the Circle K and afterwards fixed him a simple meal.

"A penny for your thoughts," he said, smiling at her gravely.

She shrugged. "Nothing special. I was just thinking how pleasant this is. I haven't built a fire for a long time. I've just been too busy."

"Tell me about your father," he said softly, putting an arm around her shoulders.

She shook her head, unable to talk for the tears that threatened to choke her every time she thought about her father.

"Hilary." His voice was patient and gentle. "You've kept all this bottled up inside you for too long. Let it out now. You must. For your own sake."

And suddenly the words came pouring out and she was telling him the whole story, about her promises to Mama, and buying the ranch, about Papa's death. Even about Justin's betrayal.

"So it was the wager with Justin that started your father toward the end."

"Yes." By this time she was crying against his shirtfront. It was a luxury she had never known, to be able to give way to grief while being held in comforting arms.

"No wonder the man looked at me like that," he said, patting her shoulder. "He's jealous."

Hilary lifted her head to look at him. She had not exactly told Taylor that she and Justin were lovers. And she hadn't told him about that night in Kentucky when she had lost all her sense. She was ashamed of that night, of what she had done. He remained quiet for a few minutes and she closed her eyes and rested there, against his chest, feeling safe and protected.

"You've been having it rough," he said finally, smoothing her tousled hair with strong gentle fingers. "All these problems. And for such a long time."

"I survived."

The arms around her tightened. "I'm aware of that, my dear. But you shouldn't have to handle all this alone."

She managed a weak little smile. "Mama always said that adversity builds character."

He didn't smile in return. "Perhaps. But in your case I think you've had more than enough. Listen, why don't you consolidate these loans? Let me advance you the money. You can pay it back in easy payments." He smiled at her fondly. "Whatever terms you like."

"Thank you, Taylor." She sat erect, wiping at her face with the handkerchief from her back pocket. "That's very kind of you, but I can't do it. I can't be beholden to you."

"Must you think of it that way?" he asked.

"I'm afraid so." She met his eyes squarely. "I have to do this on my own. And really, things are much better now. I have my salary as Justin's trainer, and there'll be horses coming in to work with. Like the ones you're sending."

He sighed. "I was afraid you would act this way. But I respect your wishes." His eyes held hers, warm and friendly. "You're a woman to be respected."

He searched her face. "You must know that I'm not here simply because of the horses."

She nodded. This was the moment she'd been dreading, the moment when he would ask questions for which she had no answers. "I . . . I sort of got the idea. I don't suppose you send bushels of roses to all your trainers."

Her little attempt at humor didn't reach him, and she lapsed into an uneasy silence.

"I know this is very short notice," he continued. "We haven't known each other long. But you must be aware that I'm very attracted to you." He shook his head. "You wouldn't believe what I went through, how many strings I had to pull, meetings I had to rearrange, to get this time to spend with you."

She nodded. She knew he must have many heavy responsibilities.

"I don't want to rush you," he said. He grinned briefly. "Well, maybe I do. But I want to be fair. My intentions are quite serious, Hilary. And quite permanent. I don't go in for quickie romances. If I love a woman, I mean to offer her everything I have, including my name."

His eyes, staring into hers, were so strong, so warm. Oh, she wanted to love him, too. To live with him forever, safe and secure.

"I'm beginning to fall in love with you, Hilary. And I want to know how you feel about me."

"I..." She tried to be as truthful as possible; she owed him that. "I like you a lot, Taylor. An awful lot. You're a great person. You're fun to be with. You make me feel attractive and worthwhile. You listen to what I say and you respect my opinions. I already love you as a friend." She paused, not knowing how to go on.

"Is it Justin? Are you still in love with him?"

Color flooded her face. She owed him the truth. "Yes, I suppose I am. What we had was wonderful. But it was so short. And so long ago." She winced, thinking of that night in Kentucky that had not been long ago.

She took Taylor's hands in hers and returned his gaze earnestly. "I want to be honest with you, Taylor. Up to now, Justin has been the only man in my life. I love him and I know that's wrong. After what he did to Papa." She shook her head. "But I still feel obligated to work out the year for him. And when I'm with him..." She faltered, not knowing how to say this without hurting Taylor.

"When you're with him, you want him," he said quietly.

"Yes." He was so good, making things easier for her. "But I don't *want* to want him." She hurried on. "I'm ashamed to have such feelings for a man who did what he did."

His eyes darkened and he sighed. "Well, I suppose none of this has to be decided tonight. We have time, don't we?"

"Yes, Taylor. Thank you." Wiping at her face, she managed a watery smile. "P. Taylor Morris, you're a wonderfully kind man."

His smile was rueful. "Don't give me any wings, Hilary. This is important to me, too. The kind of decision I'm asking of you is not to be made lightly. Marriage, in my book at least, is for a lifetime."

"In mine, too," she replied simply.

He kissed her then, softly and tenderly. And she responded, feeling the goodness of him, his warmth and strength, his kindness and understanding. She wanted to love him; she wanted to very much.

They sat there together for some time, his arms around her, looking into the fire. Until finally Taylor said, "I'm afraid I'm going to have to head for my bed, Hilary. Jet lag is catching up with me."

"Of course." She got to her feet. He already had his things in the room she had given him. Would he suggest that she join him there? And if he did, what would she say?

She wanted to love him. It was surely the sensible thing to do. She couldn't go on like this, loving a man who was as wrong for her as Justin was. She had to do something to break the spell.

Some of this must have shown in her face, for Taylor smiled gently. "I'll sleep alone tonight, Hilary. Much as I'd like to have your company. I want you to have time to think."

"Yes." She nodded, vaguely aware that she felt relief. With their arms around each other's waists, they moved toward the hall.

He kissed her once more, his lips warm and tender, then he went into his room. "See you in the morning," he said before he shut the door. "Remember, you promised me a picnic on the prairie."

"I remember. Good night."

Moving slowly toward her own room, Hilary frowned thoughtfully. This was not how she had imagined the evening would go. She had never thought she would tell him about Papa's problems. And she had never, ever meant to tell him about Justin.

But there was something about Taylor, something so good, that it just seemed natural to share her troubles with him. That was one thing she had never done with Justin. Oh, she had shared her everyday problems, but the really important things such as her worries over Papa, she had struggled with alone. That had probably been a mistake. But at the time it had seemed the right thing to do.

Instinctively she felt that with Taylor there would be no secrets. He knew about Papa already, of course, and he knew about Justin. Probably he had guessed that before she told him. She would not be able to deceive him about her feelings for Justin.

She was glad about that. A marriage built on a lie would never work. But how about one built on liking and not love? Would they be able to make that work?

Wearily she stripped off her clothes and slipped into bed. This, she thought, would be a good night to take another of those sleeping pills she'd used in Kentucky. She didn't have any now, of course. Those were the first ones she had ever used. But she badly needed some sleep, and Taylor wasn't going to come pounding on her door as Justin had. Taylor would always respect her wishes.

She sighed deeply. If only she knew what those wishes were.

The next morning she and Taylor rode out to the summer prairie. The buffalo grass swayed gently in the breeze, the sky shone a beautiful brilliant blue and from the distance a meadowlark trilled a happy song.

"The prairie is quite a place," Taylor remarked as he looked around him. "It's big out here."

Hilary laughed. "That's the first thing that everyone notices. That and—"

"The silence," Taylor interrupted. "I've been wondering what was so strange about the place. There are no traffic sounds, even distant ones in the background."

"Yes," said Hilary softly. "I love it. It's so peaceful."

They rode for some time in silence, appreciating the beauty around them. Then Taylor turned to her. "You amaze me, Hilary Benson."

She stared at him. "Why? There's nothing unusual about me."

His laughter was hearty. "You're very unusual. You handle a rogue horse as though he were a little puppy."

Hilary laughed. "I didn't do anything unusual then, either. BB isn't a rogue."

He smiled at her warmly. "I saw you go into the pasture. I watched you standing there, your back to that horse, that silly handkerchief sticking out of your pocket." He shook his head. "I couldn't believe you'd turn your back on a strange stallion. I watched with my heart in my mouth, I can tell you."

He chuckled. "If I'd been closer, I'd have come charging in there and yanked you out."

Hilary's smile was relaxed. "There was no need. I had nothing to fear from the stallion. I knew that."

Taylor shook his head. "I don't understand how you do it. Have you no fear at all?"

"No," Hilary said. "Why should I? No horse has ever hurt me."

"Such faith." Taylor shook his head.

"In their case it has always been justified."

"And your faith in people hasn't?" he asked softly.

"Yes." He was right about that. "People are much harder to deal with."

"And to love," said Taylor, his eyes searching hers.

"Yes," she agreed, trying for lightness. "And to love."

His eyes held hers for another long moment, then moved away. "Are those cottonwoods I see over there?" he asked.

"Yes. There's a little stream."

"Shall we go that way?"

"If you like." It was not a place she would have chosen to take Taylor to, the place where she and Justin had first made love. But she could hardly tell him that.

He clucked his mount into an easy canter, and she did the same with Brandy. Together they loped across the prairie, pulling up at the little grove of trees.

Taylor swung down. "Can we eat lunch here?"

"Sure." It was the obvious place, she thought as he came swiftly toward her and lifted her down. His hands were strong on her waist and for a moment as he looked down at her she thought he would kiss her, but he gave her only a brief hug.

"I'll get our lunch." It was time, she thought as she untied the saddlebag, time to forget about Justin and what they had had together, time to build a new life. A new life with Taylor.

When the saddlebag was loose, Taylor slung it over his shoulder. "Shall we make a place over there, by the water?"

"Yes." In spite of her resolution not to let the place bother her, she was pleased to see that they were a little downstream from where she and Justin had been.

She spread out the food, the sandwiches and fruit she had packed, the chocolate cake Cookie had sent home with her.

Taylor smiled. "I can't remember the last time I went on a picnic. You're very good for me, Hilary."

"And you for me," she replied simply.

They had finished their sandwiches and Taylor was peeling an orange for her, when Brandy nickered. "Someone's coming," Hilary said.

Taylor looked up. "Yes, I see him."

She didn't have to ask who it was; that sixth sense of hers warned her that it was Justin who was approaching.

"Hello, Justin." Taylor seemed entirely at ease.

Fighting down an urge to scramble to her feet, Hilary turned. Sitting astride Golden Boy, Justin looked gigantic. He did not dismount; he simply sat there and looked down at them like some avenging spirit. "Having a picnic?" he asked, making the word sound somehow obscene.

"Yes," said Taylor, still seemingly at ease. "Would you care to join us? We have plenty of food."

He can't be that much at ease, Hilary thought, her heart threatening to choke her. Taylor was no fool. He could certainly see that Justin was angry, and barely keeping that anger in check.

"No, thank you," Justin replied. "I have things to do." Again there was that tone of accusation.

"Yes," replied Taylor equitably. "I know how that is. There are always things to do."

For a moment the two men stared at each other. The air almost crackled between them, so tense was the atmosphere. Justin's stallion shifted uncomfortably, aware of his rider's anger and made uneasy by it.

Hilary's heart pounded in her throat and she found it difficult to breathe. She had never seen Justin so angry. He seemed to be literally choking his teeth to keep himself under control.

Dear God, she thought, they can't fight each other. Not these two who mean more to me than anyone else in the world.

Finally, when Hilary thought she would scream with the tension, Taylor reached casually for another piece of fruit and broke the eye contact. Justin's eyes swung to her. It took all her strength to meet his gaze, but she refused to look away. She had done nothing wrong.

His eyes burned into hers. They were cloudy and dark, full of anger. She longed to leap to her feet, to throw herself into his arms. But she forced herself to sit quietly, to return his gaze steadily. The attraction was still there between them, but she could not respond to it. Loving him didn't change anything. This was still the man who had ruined her father. She had to remember that.

He held her stare for long moments, his eyes boring into hers as though he would pry out the secrets of her soul. Her breath caught in her throat, her heart pounded madly. Then, his face still set in hard, stern lines, he reared the stallion, whirled him around and galloped away. The echo of his pounding hooves receded into the distance.

Taylor smiled. "Well, the quarter horse is known for his quick start," he commented dryly. But then he caught sight of her eyes and his smile faded. "I'm sorry about this, Hilary. I never wanted my visit to cause you pain."

She shook her head. "It's not your fault, Taylor. It's between Justin and me."

"Yes," said Taylor quietly. "It's between Justin and you."

For a long moment there was silence. She picked a purple prairie aster and stared at it absently.

Then Taylor chuckled. "Did I ever tell you what my horrible first name is?"

"No," she said. Thanking him silently with her eyes, she managed a shaky smile. "Are you sure you want to divulge such a terrible secret?"

"Yes," he said. "But you must promise..." He shook his head. "No, there's no use asking that of you."

"Asking what of me?" she replied, already feeling a little better.

"Asking you not to laugh when you hear it. No, No." He raised a hand. "Don't promise me. It really *is* funny."

"Taylor, what is it?"

"My whole name," he said, his eyes dancing with amusement, "is Phineas Taylor Morris."

"Phineas? Your name is really Phineas?"

"Really," he replied. "You don't think I'd make up a name like that?"

"No, no." She was smiling now. How could she not smile with him making such an effort to help her?"

"And you can see why I don't use it."

"Yes." She couldn't help herself; the laughter spilled out. "Oh, Taylor, how could they? How could they have pinned such a name on a defence-less baby?"

He laughed with her. "It's a very old name. With a long history in the family. Fortunately I was a husky boy, able to protect myself." He smiled thoughtfully. "Sometimes it pays to be handy with your fists."

Ten

—

Taylor left the next morning. His smile was just a little sad as he said his goodbyes. "I haven't written us off yet, Hilary. Time can work miracles. And if it doesn't, if you and I never become a team, I will still have gained a great deal from knowing you."

"But someone else could have taught you about horses," she began.

He put a finger across her lips. "Hilary, Hilary, you underestimate yourself. You know a lot more about people than you realize. You've given me back something I thought I'd lost forever."

She gazed up into his eyes. "I don't understand," she said. "I don't understand at all."

"You've given me back my taste for life," he said solemnly. "My joy in living. After Mary Lou died, I immersed myself in my work. It became everything for me. Until I met you. You've helped me to recover my normal human feelings. And for that I'll be forever grateful, no matter what else happens or doesn't happen between us."

Hilary kissed his cheek. "I said it before, Taylor, but I'll say it again. You are a wonderful man."

Grooming the mares and playing with the foals, Hilary finally made the day pass. It seemed quite long and lonely without Taylor's company. And after dinner she couldn't stand the oppressive silence of the living room.

If she hadn't told Jeb to take the day off after he'd dropped Taylor at Justin's strip, she would at least have had some human company. But, since she hadn't, there was only one thing left to do. She picked up the portable radio and a book and set off for the stable where two mares with new foals were still in stalls. A dog might be a man's best friend, she thought with an attempt at humor, but for her it was a horse every time.

The mares nickered their greetings, and Hilary went to each of them to say hello before she turned on the radio and settled herself on a blanket in the straw to read.

The novel was useless, of course: she simply couldn't get interested in anyone else's problems. As dusk fell outside she gave up the attempt. Lying back in the straw, she let her mind go where it would. And it always went back to Justin. Justin loved her. She could hardly deny that. And she loved him.

But there was still the matter of Papa. The dusk outside turned to darkness and the rising moon eventually shone in through the windows, but Hilary didn't move. Over and over again she replayed her memories of the past. If only Justin were sorry. If only he would admit to what he had done. But no, he kept insisting that it wasn't his fault, that Papa had been a drunk and a gambler all along.

Justin didn't gamble anymore. She heard all the town gossip through Jeb, and she knew he'd quit after the accident. Quit cold, so they said. No one even approached him for a game now. And he didn't drink, either. Jeb said he'd given that up, too.

Hilary lay back in the straw and tried to relax. If there could be some chance for them . . .

The stable door flew open with a bang that startled the drowsing horses and brought Hilary trembling to her feet.

"What . . . what do you want?" she asked. Justin was still angry. Even in the moonlight she could see that.

He took a step toward her. "What do you think?" he said grimly. "I want you."

She knew suddenly what she must do. She could no longer deny what was between them. Hadn't

Justin said it wasn't his fault? Over and over he'd told her that. But she hadn't believed him. She'd believed Papa instead. Papa who had amassed all those terrible gambling debts, none of which had been with Justin, none except the wager about the horses. That meant Papa must have been gambling with others. Often. And a lot. Her grandparents had told her over and over that Papa was not to be trusted with money, that the ranch must remain in her name. Why hadn't she believed them? Why had she insisted on blaming Justin?

"Justin, I . . ."

"I don't want any excuses," he said gruffly. "No words. I just want you. Now."

In a few long strides he crossed the distance between them. His hands closed roughly on her upper arm and he gave her a little shake.

"Don't tell me any lies," he growled, his eyes burning into hers. "I want you and I know you want me."

She tried to answer him, but his arms went around her, crushing her to him, and his mouth covered hers savagely, bruising her lips. She struggled in his arms, not to escape him, but to get her own arms free, to be able to put them around him.

His tongue forced her mouth open, taking possession, claiming sovereignty of her whole trembling body, a body that already twisted in anticipation of ecstasy.

When he released her mouth, her flesh was quivering, her knees so weak they would hardly hold her erect. His hands went to the front of her shirt, roughly pulling it open to expose her bra and the breasts that rose and fell heavily in time with her breathing.

He jerked the shirt down over her shoulders, pinning her arms against her sides. His free hand plunged into the front of her bra, cupping the breast that swelled there, yearning for his touch. As he bent his head and covered the nipple with his eager mouth, she moaned aloud.

He raised his head and through heavy-lidded eyes she glimpsed the triumph on his face. Then he was stripping off her shirt and bra, ripping open and discarding his own shirt. Their bare flesh met and she moaned again. It had been so long since Kentucky. So very long.

He pulled her down onto the blanket, his hands on her belt buckle, his mouth on her breasts, her shoulder, her throat.

The buckle loosened in his hands. In a kind of frenzy he stripped her of boots and jeans and panties, pulled off his own boots and stepped out of his jeans.

She wanted him, she thought hazily, she wanted him and she loved him. They had to work this thing out. They couldn't be separated any longer.

His body covered hers with a force that knocked the breath from her. This was no leisurely soothing lovemaking such as she had imagined with Taylor. This mating overflowed with raw, surging power. Sexual energy practically crackled in the air around them.

His kisses were driving her mad. Savage and passionate, they bruised her lips and made her ache for him grow ever stronger. He buried his hands in the mass of her hair, his kisses burning her forehead, her cheeks, the pulse at her throat, her shoulders. His lips only brushed hers, never staying long enough to satisfy her, only long enough to make the ache inside her grow and grow, until it seemed almost unbearable.

His tongue teased her lips, coaxing them open, then darting inside to plunder the sweet depths. Her body arched to meet his, quivering with the intensity of her need.

He entered her, finally, driving her down against the blanket into the straw. Driving into the very depths of her being, reaching the vault of her hidden treasure, setting fire to the body that now belonged, in the deepest sense of the word, not to her, not to him, but to both of them.

Her fingers clutched at his shoulders as he drove deeper and deeper, as her ache and her need grew and grew until she thought she would burst with its urgency, with this terrible need.

He lifted his head and his mouth ravaged hers. His teeth teased her bottom lip, covered her mouth with a crushing kiss.

Then his head fell against her shoulder, his breath coming in great gasps as he collapsed against her. Her body exploded into a million little shimmering pieces of contentment that slowly floated back to earth.

For a long delicious moment he didn't move. Now we'll be able to talk, she thought happily.

The next second he had rolled off her and was getting to his feet. She stared up at him, trying to marshall her senses. "Justin . . ."

He climbed into his shorts, yanked his jeans up over slim hips and jerked on his boots. "Don't bother with any excuses," he said bitterly, his jaw clenching. "I just thought I'd refresh your memory. How is Taylor? Is he as good as that?"

She felt as though she'd been doused in freezing water, and her anger erupted. "Who the hell do you think you are?" she demanded, grabbing up her shirt and shoving her arms into it. "You have no right to talk to me like that!"

She reached for her panties, uncomfortably aware that her nakedness gave him some kind of psychological advantage.

"I used to have the right!" he bellowed. "Before Taylor took over."

"No! Oh no, you didn't!" She yanked on her jeans and scrambled to her feet.

"The hell I didn't." His skin was livid, his dark eyes two burning holes in his face. "Your old man ruined things for us."

"Justin!" She could see the pain on his face, the lines of anguish around his mouth.

"I should have known when I found you and Taylor together at *our* place." His voice was scathing. "You couldn't just do it anywhere. You had to take him to our place on the prairie." His eyes blazed. "Was I second that night in Kentucky? Had he already left your room when I got there?"

Her own temper blazed. He had no right to talk to her like this. "I don't see what you're being so high and mighty about. You were with Mitzi Drummond. You were with her for a long time before you came to me." Her heart was pounding and her hands closed into fists. "What were you doing with her all that time?"

"That's none of your damn business," he growled. "The whole Kentucky trip was a mistake. Hiring you as a trainer was a mistake. Thinking you loved me was a mistake." The bitterness of his words etched itself into her heart. "You look down at Mitzi. But at least she's honest. She admits what she's after. But you lie all the time. I've had it," he cried, jamming his hat on his head. "You're fired. The wager is paid."

"But Golden Lady..." she began.

"When you're through training her, someone will come for her." In his anger his Northern accent was even more pronounced. "I don't want to see you again. I've had all I can handle. I'm going to put the ranch up for sale."

"Justin..." But he was gone, slamming the door behind him with a force that set the mares to shuffling nervously. For once in her life, Hilary had no thought for her horses. She fell to her knees on the rumpled blanket and let the tears come.

Outside, Justin leaped on his roan and urged the animal toward the prairie. Anger rode with him and he pushed the horse into a punishing gallop. But after a while, he slowed its pace. After all, it wasn't Hilary he was angry with, but himself. He shouldn't have come on that way about Taylor. He just loved her so much. It made him crazy to think that guy had been with her.

And she kept insisting that he had instigated that poker game with her father, when the old man had practically twisted his arm. Sure, Justin liked to gamble. At least he had then. He'd watched the man play plenty of times, and he hadn't minded losing Golden Boy's services. The Circle K only had a dozen mares. He would gladly have given them the stallion's services free except that he knew Hilary was too proud to accept them.

He supposed he could understand how she had come to her conclusions, faulty as they were. But to blame him for the old man's boozing... That was really too much.

She should have trusted him. If she'd told him, if he'd known she wouldn't like it, he would never have played with her father. He liked to gamble, of course. It was a source of thrills. But since the night

of Bud Benson's death, he'd hated all kinds of
gambling. And as for liquor, he didn't need it,
either.

The roan whuffled softly and Justin recognized
the clump of cottonwoods ahead, the same clump
where he and Hilary had first consummated their
love. Rage roared through him again. That she had
brought Taylor *here*, here to their special place. But
his anger was brief. It would get him nowhere.

He swung down and went to sit by the water. In
spite of everything, one thing remained clear to
him. He still loved Hilary Benson. He still wanted
to marry her. And, since in his anger he had just cut
her completely out of his life, he was going to have
to do some heavy thinking.

The phone was ringing as Hilary, red-eyed and
crying, stumbled into the house and grabbed it up.
"Hello."

"Hilary, are you all right?"

She couldn't help it; the sound of Taylor's
friendly voice was too much for her. "Oh, Taylor," she sobbed. "It was awful, just awful."

"I take it you've seen Justin," he said dryly.

"Y-yes. He was here. He..." She couldn't go on.

"Sounds like he was angry," Taylor continued.
"Did you have a fight?"

"Yes. I thought..." She hesitated. It was clear to
her now that she could never marry Taylor know-

ing that she loved Justin. "I love him," she said. "I can't stop. I'm sorry, Taylor."

"I was afraid of that." She heard the disappointment in his voice. "I suppose you're sure." His voice held a tartness she had never heard before.

She swallowed a sob. "Yes, I'm sure."

"You're quite sure that you love him?"

"Yes, Taylor. I'm quite sure." She swallowed a sob. "Though I don't know what good it will do me."

"Nonsense," he said. "A resourceful woman like you will come up with something. Tell me this, do you still blame him for your father's death?"

"I . . . I don't know."

There was silence for a long moment, then Taylor spoke again. "There's something I have to tell you," he said, his voice sounding strange. "I'm not happy to have kept it from you this long. I do love you, you know. And, well...I hoped you'd get over him. I hope you won't be angry with me for not telling you sooner."

"What is it?" she asked. She could hardly believe Taylor would keep something important from her.

"You remember me telling you about the trainer? The one who told me how you greet horses?"

"Yes, I remember."

"Hilary, I talked to that man for a long time. He has friends back there. Your father was always a gambler. He hid it from you. And he always drank, too. He was just careful around you. Hilary, my dear, you have to face up to the truth. Justin is not responsible for your father's death. Your father killed himself."

"I know it was my fault," she sobbed. "I didn't keep...my promise...to Mama. I let...her down."

"Now you're really being ridiculous," he said sharply. "A child can't control another person's behavior. Not even an adult can do that. You did everything in your power to help your father. The truth of the matter is that he didn't want to be helped. And you know it now don't you? Don't you?" he insisted.

She wiped the tears from her face with the back of her hand. "Yes, Taylor." Things were finally beginning to make sense. "I think I do. Finally. Thank you. You've been a wonderful friend to me."

"Have been?" he asked, his voice aggrieved. "Why do you speak in the past tense? I hope you're not going to shut me out of your life now. Good friends aren't easy to come by."

"You're right, Taylor. As usual." She was so relieved that he was taking it like this. He was a very good man. "I'll be glad to have you as a friend."

He chuckled. "I do hope to be asked to your wedding, if you think Justin can restrain himself. I used to be pretty good with my fists, but it's been quite a while since anyone called me Phineas."

She laughed along with him. "Of course you'll be invited. Providing there is a wedding. Remember, he said he never wanted to see me again."

"And I bet by now he's deeply regretting it. Listen, dear, I have to go now. Got to get to bed. There's a big meeting in the morning. Just hang in there, you'll make it."

Eleven

The next morning as she watched the sun come up from the warm softness of her pillows, Hilary was not sure she'd ever see Justin again, or have a wedding. She'd laid awake for hours and hours, trying to think, trying to figure out what she could say to Justin, how she could make him understand about Taylor. But every time, she came back to the fury in his voice as he yelled that she was fired, as he yelled that he never wanted to see her again. What if he had meant that? What if he had really meant it?

The ringing of the phone brought her bolt upright in her bed, her body shaking. Who could be calling at this hour? "Hello."

"It's Sandy, Miss Hilary. At the Rocking J. Have you seen the boss?"

"Last night," she stammered, trying to collect her scattered thoughts. "He was here last night."

"Yeah. That's what we thought. But he ain't come back. And, well, we're gettin' kinda worried. The prairie's a mighty big place. And if he got throwed or his horse stumbled into a prairie dog hole..."

"Yes, yes. I understand." Her mind was racing, a jumble of thoughts. Justin. Lost on the prairie. Thank God it was summer; at least he wouldn't have frozen to death. "Have you looked anywhere?"

"I just sent out a couple boys to check the trail between here and your place. Don't know what else to do. Can't hardly cover the whole prairie."

"Yes, well, that's okay. I'll saddle up and see what I can find. Don't worry. I'm sure he's all right."

"Yes, miss. I hope so. Goodbye." Sandy didn't sound convinced and neither was she. Justin knew his way around the prairie. He couldn't be just lost out there. She tugged on her clothes, trying to think. He'd been so angry when he left, probably too angry to go right back to the Rocking J. Maybe he'd gone for a ride to cool down. Maybe, like her, he'd later regretted his angry words. She sucked in her breath. Maybe he'd gone to their spot under the cottonwoods. She yanked on her boots and hurried out the door. It was someplace to start looking, at least.

Brandy picked up her agitation, turning his head to look at her quizzically, wondering what was upsetting her like this. She headed toward the prairie and clucked Brandy into an easy lope. She wanted to go faster, to gallop wildly, but she had to use a little common sense. If Justin was lying somewhere hurt, it was stupid to go galloping madly past him.

As Brandy moved along, she scanned the prairie around her anxiously. The sun was fully up now and the sky was an unclouded blue. A pair of meadow-larks trilled from nearby, and a huge jackrabbit bounded from a clump of grass as she passed—but there was no sign of Justin, or of his roan.

Dear God, she prayed. Let him be all right. Don't let him be lying someplace hurt. Not now, not when I've finally begun to see things straight.

It seemed like hundreds of miles, and endless hours to the clump of cottonwoods that marked their special place, but eventually Hilary saw the trees ahead. Her heart rose in her mouth as Brandy neared them. There was a horse, yes, Justin's roan. She could see it between the tree trunks.

As they drew nearer, Brandy slowed to a trot, then a walk. Dear God! Her heart threatened to choke her. There he was, stretched out on the grass and lying terribly still.

She leaped from Brandy's back and raced toward him. Falling on her knees in the grass, she peered anxiously down at him. "Justin! Justin! Are you hurt? Oh, darling, speak to me, please."

His face looked still and white. How badly was he hurt? A sob rose in her throat. "Justin, please! Oh, I love you! I can't lose you now."

She wanted to cradle him in her arms, but she was afraid to move him, afraid she might make his injuries worse. She bent to listen for his breath.

"Say that again."

His words startled her so that she almost lost her balance and fell on top of him. Throwing out her hands, she caught herself just in time.

His dark eyes were open, gazing up into hers. "Say you love me," he repeated.

Relief flooded over her, leaving her weak. "Of course I love you. But where are you hurt? Did you break anything? We have to get some help."

"I don't need help," he said. "I'm all right."

"But you fell. Or were thrown. You've been out all night. Sandy said . . ."

Something in his eyes gave him away. "You weren't lost at all!" she cried indignantly, suddenly seeing the whole thing. "You set this up. I bet you weren't even out all night."

"You're right," he said cheerfully. "Aside from being a little damp from lying here in the grass, I'm fine."

She scrambled to her feet. "You . . ." she cried angrily. "What a lousy thing to do. Well, you can just lie there until you rot for all I care."

She took one step toward Brandy before his hand snaked out catching her booted ankle and toppling her into his arms. "Nothing doing," he said firmly, pinning her to the prairie with his body. "Nobody leaves here until we get this thing settled."

"What thing?" She was only pretending to be angry now. He was alive and she loved him. She had him back. This was the old Justin, the one she knew she loved.

"This thing about us," he said. "I love you. I've loved you for what seems like forever. I waited and waited for you to recognize that, to admit that you love me. But you didn't. I went through hell when you and Taylor—"

"We didn't," she interrupted softly. "Taylor and I are only friends. Nothing more."

His face showed his disbelief. "But he acted like . . ."

"He loves me." She said it simply. "And he hoped we could get together. I'm sorry I blamed you for Papa's death, Justin." She touched his cheek with tender fingers. "I guess, well, I was trying so hard. And when Papa died, I really blamed myself."

Briefly, she told him of her promise to her mother. "But Taylor made me see that it wasn't my fault, that no one could have kept such a promise. The accident wasn't anybody's fault. It just happened."

He kissed her nose, her eyelids, her forehead. "My poor baby," he crooned. "So much pain."

"I was partly to blame," she admitted. "I shouldn't have pretended. I guess I always knew, somewhere, that Papa was hiding things from me. I should have confronted him with my feelings. Deception is always a bad thing."

He began to look uncomfortable.

"What is it, Justin? What's wrong?"

"I've, ah, done some things. To get you back." He looked suddenly frightened, too. "I've got to tell you, Hilary. I don't want any secrets hanging over us. I can't stand the thought of losing you again."

"Tell me," she urged, brushing the hair back from his forehead.

"Well, about the bet."

"Yes?"

"There was no salary in the deal with your father. I put that in later. You were driving yourself so hard, paying off all those debts. I couldn't take it, seeing you so tired and thin. Not eating. Not taking care of yourself. I had to do something."

He searched her face carefully. "I didn't care about getting the foal. I grabbed the chance to be with you. That's why I stuck around, why I didn't sell the Rocking J when you ditched me. Because I knew the foal was coming and I hoped and prayed it would be a filly." He stared down at her, his eyes troubled. "Can you forgive me?"

"Yes," she said unhesitantly. "I forgive you. I know you wanted to help me. I think I was sort of sick there, after Papa died. All my plans and dreams for us were ruined. I just sort of fell to pieces. I couldn't see anything right. I'm glad I got better."

"Me, too," he said fervently. "But there's one more thing I want to explain. I just wanted you to know that when that Morris character showed up and stuck to you like glue, I'm afraid I just couldn't stand seeing you with him."

"Taylor is really a very nice man." She wanted Justin to recognize that.

He nodded. "I know. But I just couldn't handle it. That's why I came pounding on your door like I did that night."

"Taylor is rather old-fashioned," she told him. "He believes in love, real love. I think," she went on softly, "that he's taught me a great deal." Seeing his dark brows begin to draw together, she laughed and reached up to plant a kiss there, between them. "There are many kinds of love, my darling Justin. Taylor is a rare and wonderful man. I treasure his friendship. I only hope that someday he can find someone to love him as much as I love you, that someday he can find the kind of happiness we have."

His brows smoothed out. "I'm for that. But speaking of love," he said softly. "I love you." He kissed her lightly. "Well, Hilary Benson, is there anything else between us? Any more confessions to make before we get married?"

"Are we getting married?" she asked happily, tracing the line of his chin with a finger and feeling the roughness of his morning whiskers.

"As soon as possible," he declared. "I want you to have a big wedding, of course. The kind every woman dreams of."

"I don't know that I want all that," she said slowly. "But there are some things we have to talk about."

"There's nothing love can't settle," he said, happily nuzzling her neck.

"Maybe so," she replied with a little chuckle. "But let's not put too big a burden on our love. Let's handle what we can ahead of time."

He sighed, but his eyes smiled down into hers. "All right. Tell me."

"I want to keep the Circle K," she said slowly. "I want to run it myself, keep it a separate operation."

He looked bewildered.

"It's mine," she said, trying to explain, "mine and Papa's. I can't let it go. I can't make it part of the Rocking J. I have to make a success of it on my own."

Justin shook his head. "You are the darndest woman. Here everything I have is yours, lock, stock and barrel, and you're worrying about a ranch. All right, darling. All right. I don't understand, but I respect your wishes. Now what about your father's debts? Will you let me pay them off?"

She shook her head. "No, Justin. I have to do that, too. But I will continue to work as your trainer and I'll let you pay me for that."

"Wonderful," he said dryly as he bent to kiss her.

"Wait, there's more."

He heaved a tremendous sigh. "What now?" he asked with mock exasperation.

"It's Taylor."

"What about Taylor?" He couldn't quite keep the anxiety out of his voice.

"He's sending me some horses with bad habits to be cured. I can't go back on the deal." She searched his face carefully, silently begging him to understand. "I want to keep Taylor as a friend," she went on. "I know that it's difficult for you. I know that it's difficult for him. But I want to do it. His friendship is valuable to me. I've had so few friends. Justin, please, please, don't ask me to give up this one."

She saw his jaw tighten, his eyes go cloudy. "You've got to trust me," she said softly, her hand on his cheek. "Without trust we have nothing. Taylor is my friend, that's *all*. I could have married him, you know, but I chose you."

His mouth covered hers hungrily for a moment. "All right," he said, his lips against her throat. "Taylor stays as a friend. I kind of like the guy myself. Now that I know you're really mine."

"For always and forever," she said, kissing the point of his stubborn chin.

"You'd better be. Anything else?" he asked, his teeth nibbling at her ear.

"There is one other thing we haven't discussed." She turned her face to kiss his cheek.

He sighed again, but he was grinning at her as he said, "At this rate we may never get married. Okay, what is it?"

"Do you like children?"

"Do you?"

"Justin Porter! Stop that this instant!" She glared up at him. "Honestly now. This is serious business we're discussing. Do you want children? And if so, how many?"

He grinned. "I always thought half a dozen was a nice round number, but if they have your hair and your eyes—"

"Oh, no," she said. "They have to be dark-haired and dark-eyed, like you."

"Well," he replied, his lips teasing one corner of her mouth. "Then we'll just have to keep going until we get some of each."

"Yes, Justin," she murmured. "That sounds good."

"If you've no other prenuptial stipulations," he whispered, biting her neck, "why don't we get up off this damp prairie and go get a marriage license?"

"Well," she replied, her mouth reaching almost up to his. "There are at least two reasons I can think of. First, the license bureau won't be open this early. And second, since we're already damp..."

"I get the idea," he murmured. "Maybe we should start child number one. Right here, in this special spot."

"I think that's a wonderful idea," she agreed, her lips soft against his. "And you're a wonderful man for thinking of it."

Silhouette Desire

Silhouette Desire Romances

TAKE 4
THRILLING SILHOUETTE
DESIRE ROMANCES
ABSOLUTELY FREE

Experience all the excitement, passion and pure joy of love. Discover fascinating stories brought to you by Silhouette's top selling authors. At last an opportunity for you to become a regular reader of Silhouette Desire. You can enjoy 6 superb new titles every month from Silhouette Reader Service, with a whole range of special benefits, a free monthly Newsletter packed with recipes, competitions and exclusive book offers. Plus information on the top Silhouette authors, a monthly guide to the stars and extra bargain offers.

An Introductory FREE GIFT for YOU.
Turn over the page for details.

As a special introduction we will send you FOUR
specially selected Silhouette Desire romances
— yours to keep FREE — when you complete
and return this coupon to us.

At the same time, because we believe that you will be so thrilled
with these novels, we will reserve a subscription to Silhouette
Reader Service for you. Every month you will receive 6 of the very
latest novels by leading romantic fiction authors, delivered direct to
your door.

Postage and packing is always completely
free. There is no obligation or commitment —
you can cancel your subscription at any time.

It's so easy. Send no money now. Simply fill in and post
the coupon today to:-

**SILHOUETTE READER SERVICE, FREEPOST,
P.O. Box 236 Croydon, SURREY CR9 9EL**

Please note: READERS IN SOUTH AFRICA to write to:-

**Independent Book Services P.T.Y.,
Postbag X3010, Randburg 2125, S. Africa**

FREE BOOKS CERTIFICATE

**To: Silhouette Reader Service, FREEPOST, PO Box 236,
Croydon, Surrey CR9 9EL**

Please send me, Free and without obligation, four specially selected Silhouette Desire Romances and reserve a
Reader Service Subscription for me. If I decide to subscribe, I shall, from the beginning of the month following my
free parcel of books, receive six books each month for £5.94, post and packing free. If I decide not to subscribe I
shall write to you within 10 days. The free books are mine to keep in any case. I understand that I may cancel my
subscription at any time simply by writing to you. I am over 18 years of age.
Please write in BLOCK CAPITALS.

Name _____

Address _____

_____

_____ Postcode _____

SEND NO MONEY — TAKE NO RISKS

*Remember postcodes speed delivery. Offer applies in U.K. only
and is not valid to present subscribers. Silhouette reserve the right
to exercise discretion in granting membership. If price changes
are necessary you will be notified.
Offer limited to one per household. Offer expires July 31st
1986.*

EP18SD